HOW TO WALK
ON WATER

AND OTHER STORIES

HOW TO WALK
ON WATER
AND OTHER STORIES

Rachel Swearingen

newamericanpress

Milwaukee, Wis.

newamericanpress

© 2020 by Rachel Swearingen

Printed in the United States of America

ISBN 9781941561225

Interior design by Jessica Miller

Cover design by Alban Fischer
https://albanfischerdesign.com

"Felina" appeared previously in *Mississippi Review*; "Notes to a Shadowy Man" in *Cimarron Review*; "Boys on a Veranda" in *Connecticut Review*; "Edith Under the Streetlight" in *The Massachusetts Review*; "Mitz's Theory of Everything Series" in *Agni*, and reprinted in *New Stories from the Midwest, 2013*; "The Only Thing Missing Was the Howling of Wolves" in *Kenyon Review*; "A Habit of Seeing" in *Fifth Wednesday*; "How to Walk on Water" in *The Missouri Review*; *and* "Advice for the Haunted" in *VICE*.

For ordering information, please contact:
Ingram Book Group
One Ingram Blvd.
La Vergne, TN 37086
Phone: (800) 937-8000
Fax: (800) 876-0186
https://www.ingramcontent.com
orders@ingrambook.com

For event and media requests, please visit:
New American Press
www.newamericanpress.com

For John

CONTENTS

FELINA

for Louise Bourgeois

WHEN FELINA TOLD ARTHUR SHE COULD ARRANGE A WOMAN'S hair to resemble a waterfall or a parking garage, that she could arrange fruit like a woman lounging in space, he wasn't really listening. He was distracted by her short skirt and grey fedora. He had noticed her all the way across The Factory nightclub, stacking candleholders and cocktail glasses into an elaborate tower. He asked her what she was doing. That's when she told him he was looking at the Next Big Thing. "I've got ideas," she said. "It would blow your mind."

Arthur worked as an account executive for an investment management firm that had been sold twice in the past three years—he didn't think anything could blow his mind anymore, but he was open to the possibility. He bought her a drink and sat across from her as she cleared the table and draped it with black silk from an attaché case. She made folds in the material, directed the light so it cast shadows and drew the eye past melting ice cubes to the imprint of lipstick on a glass. "Most of the world takes light for granted," she said. "And shadow for that matter too."

He imagined the two of them back in his apartment, tangled

together in his sheets. He leaned back so he wouldn't seem too eager and looked around the room.

"It's haunted, you know," she said. Her fedora slipped back to reveal a wide forehead and black bangs. She had a squarish face and dark blue eyes that reminded Arthur of a Laplander princess in *National Geographic*. "At night, when they're closing up, the bartenders hear machines whirring and see women in old-fashioned dresses working. It used to be a textile mill."

Arthur asked her about her own work, about where she grew up, about what she liked to do in the city. She answered vaguely. She'd spent part of her childhood in France. She assisted photographers "here and there," and sometimes dressed department store windows. She asked her own questions: Did Arthur get that complexion working under fluorescent lights? Did he believe in ghosts? Was he one of those people who *was* what he did, or *did* what he did, or *did something other* than he did?

He took too long to answer. With another kind of woman he would boast about his largest accounts. He would pretend he loved the thrill of the market, the ups and downs, the rushing in to work before the bell. He would brag about trips to Taiwan and India, about mountain biking and hang-gliding, things he hadn't done in a long time and had never enjoyed. He stared at Felina. He leaned over and tipped her fedora down over her forehead and said, "There's no such thing as ghosts."

Felina pulled the silk off the table. "That's what you think," she said. She snapped the fabric in the air and wrapped it around herself so that only her eyes peeked out. "I should go."

Arthur followed her outside. "I didn't get your number," he said, when she turned to get into a cab.

"In your pocket," she said. And then she was gone.

Arthur felt his breast pocket. She must have slipped in the card when she draped fabric around his shoulders to show how folds give the impression of girth. *Felina Jones, Visualist*, the card read in tall avant-garde letters.

He waited two days before calling her, leaving a voicemail with his phone number and asking if she would like to get coffee sometime. Maybe she wouldn't be interested in a guy who spent his time analyzing profits and losses. It was a terrible time to be an investor. In less than six months all of his accounts had tanked. Clients called and e-mailed, and threatened to change firms. The longtime ones were the most difficult, not because they complained more, but because Arthur knew about the kids they were putting through college, about their divorces and lost jobs, their re-marriages, the failing health of parents, and their own horrific illnesses. Hart Shultz, a manufacturer forced into early retirement, had been calling for days. Arthur sent an e-mail instead of returning his call. He sent the same e-mail to all his clients, told them that long-term investment was just that, *long-term*, and in "these trying times" it was important not to lose faith, that "Smith and Wao Investments has always been committed to smart growth for the smart investor."

Then he skipped lunch and walked the city looking in department store windows for Felina's drapes and folds.

When she finally returned his call, Arthur was surprised by how different her voice sounded—low and winsome, yes, winsome was the word. She'd rather not get coffee, she said. He suggested dinner, and she said, "No, come to my apartment? At ten?"

She lived on the other side of the city in what used to be an old Bohemian neighborhood, but was now filled with bodegas and *cuchifrito* shops, and was lately overrun with young artist types. He took the subway, emerged to a mix of rundown apartment buildings, refurbished warehouses, and new cafés. He walked several blocks until he found her building, a three-story, turn-of-the-century brownstone. He buzzed her apartment, but no one came. He called Felina's number, and finally she appeared at a second-floor window. "The door's broken," she said. "Just come up."

He climbed a dark stairwell that smelled of Chinese food and something fragrant he couldn't identify. Though it was late, he heard a woman singing in a first-floor apartment, warming her voice up with "mi, mi, mi, mi, mi." He rounded the corner and opened a door to the second floor and a hallway of worn carpet and peeling wallpaper. He worried suddenly that Felina still lived with her parents, that he'd spend the night sitting next to a grandmother who couldn't speak English. He knocked and heard soft pattering, and then the door opened to Felina in a 50s cocktail dress and flowered apron. She curtsied and pulled her skirt to one side, pointed her tongue in the other.

"Can I take your hat?" she asked.

"I must have left it on the train," he joked.

"Here," she said, and she took a hat off a rack next to the door and handed it to him—the very same fedora she wore the night they met. The very same hat he had daydreamed about seeing on her naked body.

Arthur put the hat on and tipped it at her. He felt debonair as he stepped into her dark apartment. She had lined the edges of the foyer with Christmas lights so it reminded him of an airport runway.

"Let me take your hat," she said again.

He handed it to her and followed her past a hideaway kitchen to a small living area. Felina walked with her legs slightly bowed, her shoulders tucked back like a dancer.

What little furniture she had was draped with sheets. In one corner, she had positioned a photographer's light stand, directed its reflector over a shrouded ottoman that displayed a still life of fruit around an impossible tower of crackers.

"Sit down," she said. "Take off your shoes."

Arthur sat down on the floor. He tucked his legs under his knees and tried not to upset the tower. She was like a child preparing for a tea party. She made funny noises with her tongue against her teeth as she busied herself behind him, pulling out liquor bottles and reaching deep into the cabinet next to him. She presented Arthur with a bottle shaped like a goose.

"What is it?" Arthur said.

She kneeled and poured clear liqueur into two coffee cups. "Drink it, you'll like it, said the cat to Alice. So you're an Arthur?"

"My grandfather's name. I never even met him."

"I like it," she said. "I don't know any other Arthurs."

He hated his name. It sounded like an old man's name. The liqueur had a horrid smoky sweet taste. "This is very nice," he said, and it was almost true, the taste was something he might grow used to and perhaps even like.

"It's made from potatoes," she said. "The Poles. They make everything from potatoes. Once when I was in Poland I sat on a chair made out of potatoes. We later ate it in a goulash."

He laughed, but she blinked at him as if she were waiting for him to offer his own, funnier, story. He had never been to Poland. His last trip was to Mumbai for a friend's wedding, a spectacular three-day affair, ending with a nontraditional gala at a hotel in the city. Arthur had never seen so much food and after two days of dry celebration and unrelenting heat, of offending various relatives with his ignorance of custom, he stationed himself at the hotel bar and drank his fill of rum. It had been a terrible year, the culmination of several terrible years. He tried to convince one of the guests to come to bed with him, and when she declined, he worked on the groom's oldest sister and then her aunt. Some men from the groom's party escorted him up to his room above the reception hall and told him to stay put, but he wandered out into the streets, perfectly aware he was getting lost, that anything could happen, that he might disappear forever. He stumbled through narrow alleys, past women and children in doorways, men gambling, smoking, arguing, pushing carts of garbage. The crowds thickened and a group of kids pushed him down a stairwell and mugged him. He hadn't fought back. He just lay there, finally crawling into the entryway of a tobacco shop and passing out in his own vomit. In the morning, he had to find his way back to the hotel and ask his friend for help getting a new passport and money. Arthur hadn't heard from him since.

Felina stared at him and chewed at her bottom lip. He needed to do something with his hands. The tower of crackers made him afraid to breathe. Not only did it have several floors, but also many open rooms with people made of toothpicks and olives inside. He plucked a tangerine from near the base and was about to peel it when he noticed a woman's figure carved into its skin. "How about some music?" he asked, setting the tangerine back down.

"Stay right there. You've got to see this," Felina said. She directed one of the lights toward the ceiling, and then pulled the sheet off the cabinet behind them and draped it over her shoulders and stood on her tiptoes. She danced through the apartment, waving her arms up and down like a delicate bat, casting winged shadows on the walls.

"Wow," he said. "That's pretty wild."

She flapped toward him, her eyes half-closed. Then she descended on him, lowered the sheet like a deflated parachute and he felt a breeze, felt her cool skin enveloping him, her arms around his neck, her lips drifting to his cheek and to his lips and the sheet closing down on them, encasing the two of them like a lovely nightmare.

"Where's your bedroom?" he whispered. The liqueur on her breath smelled like firewood. He tugged at the fabric that had gotten twisted between them and half covered Felina's face. He pulled his arm free and felt it knock against the tower, heard the crackers tumble.

Felina sat up. "Now you've ruined it," she said. She crawled over to the ottoman and squinted at the half-toppled tower and flicked it with her finger. The remaining pieces came down in a heap, olives and all.

Then she stood and gave the ottoman a swift kick with her bare foot. "That wasn't very satisfying," she said. He heard the crush of crackers as she marched to the light stand and knocked it over. Now the light shone on the opposite wall, perfectly highlighting a long, jagged crack in the plaster.

He went to her and stood the light back up. "Sorry," he said. "If it's any consolation, I thought it was amazing."

"You're not a very good liar, are you?" she said.

She tipped the lamp back on its side and focused the light on the crack, allowing the curtain from the window to cast a limpid shadow. She stepped back to examine the wall. "Hey," she said. "That's really nice. Don't you think?"

The crack spidered all the way to the ceiling and up to the light fixture at the center of the room. He watched her from the corner of his eyes. He didn't know why he chose the women he did. He couldn't decide if she was one of those posers who pretended to be artistic, or whether she really found the wall beautiful. Either way, the mood was gone.

"I should probably go," he said. "Got to be to work early tomorrow."

She went to the window and lifted the curtain and let it fall. "What we need is a fan," she said.

He looked for his shoes and told her he would call her, that he had a really nice time, and they should get together for some coffee or something sometime.

"Sure," she said, but she didn't seem interested at all. He left, and when he looked up at her window from outside, she was still standing there, playing with the light.

The next day he shared a few details of the night with his co-worker, Chuck. Chuck was a junior account manager who Arthur had taken under his wing, a likeable, freckled twenty-six-year-old with a wife and newborn, and a passion for golf. He told Chuck that Felina's apartment was like The Little Shop of Horrors. "You know what they say about spooky chicks," Chuck said, and he wiggled his fingers like he was casting a spell.

Arthur retreated to his office and took out his bag lunch and arranged it on his desk. He moved his apple behind his sandwich and then on top. He watched stock quotes race across the bottom of his computer screen and a dozen new alerts pop open. He listened to his phone vibrate itself across his desk. He wasn't very hungry. He forced himself to listen to his messages and scan his eighty-four new e-mails. Hart Schultz had called again. He demanded Arthur call him immediately; he could tell mumbo jumbo when he heard it, and maybe his father had been right when he took all his money out of the bank and stuffed his mattress.

"Listen," Schultz said, when Arthur returned his call. "You gotta be straight with me. Leona and me, we don't have twenty years. You think I can start over at sixty-six?"

"I know it looks bad," Arthur said. "You're still doing well. You've got to look at it from the right perspective. We've done everything we can to protect you. This is the best time to be in the market." Arthur didn't give Schultz a chance to mention all the shares he had earned during his career, all the shares Arthur had lost in high-risk transactions. "I'm sorry," he told him, "I'm late for a meeting."

He worked even later than usual. He wouldn't beat himself up about Schultz. Of course, Arthur might have seen the crash coming. He had even considered warning his major clients when the market reached its peak. There was nowhere to go except down. They all knew it, especially Schultz.

Arthur's screen was a maze of windows filled with colored pie charts. He answered e-mails and moved stocks and ran reports. *He* was not the market, he told himself. *He* was not to blame every time the DOW fell. He had to refocus to imagine all those slices of pie as actual money in actual accounts. The truth was he was moving air. He was part of some elaborate pattern of algorithms even the best economists couldn't comprehend.

At seven, he googled "Felina Jones" and not a single entry came up. The fact that she was a poor, unknown artist didn't surprise him. Her art had an amateur, homemade feel. He wondered just how many windows Felina had really been paid to decorate and in which sections of town, and he almost wanted to see her again.

Over three weeks passed. He didn't expect to be so undone when he heard her voice mail. "Arthur," she said. "I want you to come over. Tonight. I have a surprise for you."

When he reached her apartment, the door was ajar. He knocked softly, and then harder.

"Close your eyes and come in," she shouted from inside. "Don't open them until you can't stand it."

Arthur closed his eyes. He walked with his hands in front of him and jumped back when he bumped into what he thought was a giant man, but turned out to be a wool coat hanging from the ceiling. He almost strangled himself on a clothesline strung across the entry into the living room, loaded with nightgowns and tuxedo shirts. He opened his eyes. Felina had installed cheap floor lights and box fans and these were directed up into billowing, glowing garments. He ducked under a veil and under another line of aprons and dresses. He felt his way around the room. He wasn't sure if it was the sight of the place or the fans that gave him chills, but he pushed through the costumes and held his breath against their mustiness.

He crept back down the hallway, feeling the walls for a light switch. He finally found one and flipped on a ceiling light. When he turned around, Felina's apartment looked like the apartment of a woman too poor to use a clothes dryer. He parted a curtain of long, silk slips and entered what he discovered to be Felina's bedroom, a room filled with old photographs and other memorabilia, and Felina sitting on the edge of a brass bed, her hair longer and blonde now, parted into two braids.

"You could have waited to turn on the lights."

How small she looked in her black dress and striped stockings. And she didn't look so young after all, why she might have even been older than Arthur.

"Can you get that light again?" she said. She leaned from the bed to turn on a lamp fashioned out of a wire crinoline. The layers of yellowed ruffles cast an anemic light.

Arthur sat next to her on the bed. "I like what you did out there," he said. "It was like going back in time."

She was quiet and listening, so he went on, and after a few minutes he realized he wasn't lying anymore. He *had* had a sensation of moving through other lifetimes, of pushing through crowds. He had remembered his father's closet when he was a child, how he used to crawl inside and put his hands in his shoes, how he had loved the feel of his fingers against the depressions from his father's toes. And his mother's skirt, swishing around him. Where did that memory come from? The feel of her wet trench coat when he helped her out of it the one time he took her out for dinner with his own money when he was in high school. And he had remembered women's blouses and dresses, and skirts and pants, all falling to bathroom and bedroom and hotel floors, and the women's expressions as they undressed, their underwear and stockings pressed into the corners of his bed. And walking to work from the subway, he imagined this too, inexplicably, sometimes seeing the same face two mornings in a row.

Felina put her hand on his knee and said, "I'm sorry, Arthur, that I was so nutso with you before, that I made you go." She bit at her lip, stumbled for the right words. "You weren't saying all that just to be nice, were you?"

He put his arm around her and pulled her to him and kissed her.

"Wait," she said. She pulled bobby pins from her head and removed a wig. Her natural hair was short and a color not unlike Arthur's, a dull shade of brown. She stood and unbuttoned the back of her dress and let it slip to the floor. The light from the lamp cast a stippled pattern across her skin. She was so thin, so bare that Arthur couldn't look away.

"Not in here. I've got ghosts," she said as if the place were infested. She took his hand and led him through the hanging costumes into the main room. She knelt down on the floor and he knelt next to her. He didn't want to see her this way, naked under all those moth-eaten things that once belonged to others.

"I knew you'd come back," she said, unbuttoning his shirt. She pressed against him and grazed her lips down his chest. He was falling backwards and she was falling against him, and he could feel the rug beneath them and the hem of a night shirt brush his face. He tried to find his way back up, to push against the woman who called herself Felina, but who he was certain now had some other name and some other past he wouldn't want to know.

"Arthur," she whispered into his ear. "You get it, don't you? You really understand."

He didn't get anything, not at all. He was alone now in the back of a cab and it was four in the morning. In his hands was Felina's fedora and he was turning it around and around. The band inside had a sweat stain and a graying silk label that said Carruthers and Sons. Felina had given it to him on the way out, and he had propped it on his head and bowed. He had awoken tangled with her in a pile of clothing and had to get out of there. Her legs were ungodly white and skinny. When those legs were clasped around him and he had his hands on her narrow hips, he felt she was taking him out to sea. He wanted to be both wrapped in those legs right now and to be very far away, to never, not ever go back to her apartment with all its dingy props.

He was certain she was not a display artist at all. She was probably a waitress or had some other line of work he wouldn't want to know about. He took out his wallet and pulled out her business card. It was printed on thin paper and could have been from any number of machines in the city where you could plug in five dollars for a small stack. He had used one once to make prank cards for Chuck that said Professional Stuntman. What had she been doing at that club the night he met her? She had been all alone in a wig with a briefcase full of fabric, and he had just thought she was one of those cool, art-school girls. He remembered now that the cloth she had wrapped him in smelled of root vegetables. He had wanted to see what he had wanted to see, that's all. He set the hat down next to him. The cabbie had tried to start a conversation with him earlier, but Arthur hadn't been in the mood. He would give anything for a little conversation now. The streets were desolate and glowing. They entered the tunnel to the city. He didn't like tunnels at night. His eyes played tricks, the glare of the headlights on the shiny tiles that lined the tunnel made him nearly mad. If he were driving, he'd have to fight the urge to fly into the wall. Why did they always make tunnels turn, always so there was that moment when you couldn't see what was ahead at all?

At work the next day, Arthur was depressed. He pretended to have an appointment and didn't make it in until noon. When Chuck asked him about his weekend, Arthur said he stayed in. "Still not getting any, huh, pal?" Chuck said, and Arthur just shrugged. "Hey, you've got a visitor," Chuck whispered. "A real steamer. Says his name is Schultz." Arthur made his way through the section of cubicles where junior account officers like Chuck worked, back to his own cramped office. Schultz must have refused to wait in the lobby because he was sitting in a chair in front of Arthur's desk waiting for him.

He was tall and gaunt and had enormous knuckled hands. From his voice over the phone, Arthur had imagined a short man with a thick neck. "Down again," Schultz said. "I want it all out. Today. You people keep giving me the run-around."

"Let's have lunch and talk it over," Arthur said. He put his hand on Schultz's arm. "Come on, I know a great place down the street. You haven't had lunch yet, have you?"

Schultz eyed Arthur suspiciously, but he followed him to the elevator. They went down to the first floor and to the street, through crowds of people rushing to work and to school and to shops. Arthur chatted about construction on the expressway, asked Schultz what brought him into town. Schultz answered Arthur with "hard to believe anyone is building anything right now" and "you know why I'm here."

Most of the people they passed marched grimly ahead.

Even children holding onto a parent's hand had mastered the look. Arthur took Schultz to a famous diner where Schultz shook his head over the menu and said, "Twenty dollars for a pastrami and rye." They ate their sandwiches while Arthur told him about the reorganization of the company, about their new investment strategies.

"I wasn't born yesterday," Schultz said. "I know what *reorg* means. It means your business is in the crapper."

Arthur tried to placate Schultz, but finally he put down his sandwich, wiped his hands on his napkin, and pushed his plate away. "Hart," he said. "If you want to close your accounts, I can't stop you."

"That's exactly what I want," Schultz said. What a sanctimonious expression he wore, like a disappointed father. He gestured for their waiter to wrap his remaining half sandwich.

Arthur would be in with the partners by morning, out the door soon if he kept losing clients. "I'll take care of everything as soon as I get back to the office," he said. "I'm sorry."

He felt an unexpected lightness as he stood to shake Schultz's hand. He'd walk him out the door, and then no more phone calls or e-mails, no more Hart Schultz spreadsheets and disappearing pies.

Schultz, on the other hand, looked heavier. He tucked his sandwich into the pocket of his jacket and said, "Back in the day, I had to lay off a lot of good men. But this is different. Whole damn world's going to hell. Glad I won't be around long enough to see what happens."

Arthur walked him outside and watched him make his way down the street. There was something more going on with Schultz. Something about the way he carried himself as he walked away in that oversized suit in the warm weather, about how resolved he was the worst was yet to come. Maybe his wife was leaving him or one of his kids was in trouble and he needed all that money at once. Arthur wouldn't be able to explain this to the partners. He'd make promises he couldn't keep to sign on other clients to make up for the loss. He didn't want to think about it, not about Schultz, and not about his own future. He walked the opposite direction, away from the office. The day was gorgeous, and the few trees lining the streets had begun to change colors. From across the street he could see the gold brick and tightly spaced windows of the nightclub where he met Felina. When he reached the building, he brushed his hand over the brick and imagined rows of whirring spindles, towering bolts of cloth, and women, row after row of women, their hands working frantically to feed the machines.

By mid-week, he couldn't stop thinking of her. She had to be waiting for him to call. He couldn't make himself do the things he ought to do. He'd been put on notice by the firm. He had one quarter to turn things around. At lunch, he walked with Chuck to the deli and as Arthur listened to him prattle on about the way his wife spent money and lorded the difficult birth of their son over him, Arthur thought of Felina sitting on the edge of her bed, her hands folded in her lap, her braids askew, the way she had blinked up at him when he turned on the light, and he wanted to hear her voice, he wanted to feel her cold bony feet on his back.

So he called and left a message. He stammered about dinner, how nice it would be to take her out to a restaurant, maybe she could meet him downtown and he'd show her his place.

But she didn't call him back, not until several weeks later, and by then he was angry. Why was she stringing him along?

"I'm not stringing you along, Arthur. I've been very busy. I've been busy *for you*."

He pretended not to hear. He didn't want any more surprises.

"Tonight, Arthur," she said. "But not before ten. I need time to get ready."

By the time he arrived at her building, he no longer had the desire to climb her stairs. He took them slowly and when he reached her apartment door, he saw that she had left it open a crack. This time there were no lights, not on the floor or in the living room, no fans, and no clothes hanging from the ceiling. The apartment was warm and dark and quiet. "Felina?" he called. He opened the door to her bedroom and felt for the switch. There was tape over it. He staggered forward with his arms in front of him feeling for the bed. His hand felt the back of a leg, a lifeless leg, and he jumped. He felt for the lamp nearby and when he turned it on, he was horrified to see figures under the bedding. Don't look, he told himself as he lifted a blanket. But even then as his brain took in two prone and forms, stuffed, sewn coarsely with white thread, he was aware of someone behind him. He turned and there, pressed into the corner, was another crude figure.

He backed out of the room and fumbled through the hallway, through a myriad of copulating forms, in twos and threes and alone, all headless, some armless, one wearing a fake leather leg. He told himself, in a gallery this would not be terrifying, this would be art. "Felina!" he called.

She was nowhere to be found. He slunk down against the wall in the living room and thought of her sitting for days on end, sewing and stuffing trunks and limbs. Each time a car passed the headlights flashed across three forms twisted together at the middle of the room and he remembered lying awake as a child, hearing his parents making love quietly in their room one night before his father died. He remembered his mother cleaning, all through his childhood, cleaning and tabulating grocery receipts and bills, saving every scrap of paper and string. *You gotta take a paper route*, she would say. *We've got to eat. Here, Arthur, I found you a job washing dishes. Mr. Carlotti wants you to shovel his walk.* She herself worked three jobs, even knitted scarves and strung beads and sold them in front of the train station before the holidays. *They'll throw us out, we don't work harder.* She wouldn't let him quit school, just told him only deadbeats needed sleep. When he was eighteen and considering the Army just to get away from her, she pressed a bankbook into his hand and said, "Arthur, this is for you. Now you can go to school. Now you'll be a big man like your father wanted you to be." Fifty thousand dollars, a fortune in those days. She died six months later, a tumor in her abdomen the size of a grapefruit.

"Felina, if you can hear me, I've had enough. I'm going."

"What's the matter, Artie," she said. She emerged from

the tangle of figures in the middle of the room, wearing a black leotard. She tore a nylon stocking off her head so her hair stood up from the static. "Don't you like it?"

"You're delusional," Arthur said. "You need help." He stood and walked to the door.

She followed him. "But you haven't seen it all."

Arthur opened the door and ran down the stairs. He recognized, suddenly, the feel of the wood railing. He was afraid that if he turned around he would see his mother poke her head out a door and call for him. A woman was singing scales again in the first-floor apartment, while a man shouted, "Extend. Extend. From the diaphragm!"

He opened the door to the street and breathed in the night air. It smelled of rain and the street glistened. Cars were parked on either side and one had a ticket on its window, and all the way down the block he saw lights in apartments and knew people were inside, listening to music and watching television, and talking to people they loved and people who drove them crazy. He stood in the middle of the road and looked up at Felina's windows, knowing she was there, peering down at him.

"Wait, Arthur," she called. "This is the one I told you about."

She moved away and he heard some metallic clamoring. Then a light appeared in the window, and he saw them, tangerines and apples, bananas and a pineapple, all dangling in the frame of the open window.

"Can you see it?" she shouted.

He could, just barely, if he squinted and blurred the edges

of the fruit, if he ignored the glinting of the fishing line—a woman lounging in space. He thought of Mumbai, the night he had lain in the street, garbage strewn all around him, the sounds of bicycles and sandaled feet and someone far away praying. How beautiful everything had been for those few moments when he was without his wallet and his name, and he didn't even think about the value of such things.

Felina came down and together they stared up at the window. "That's the thing about lighting," she said, as the pineapple tilted slowly and her lounging woman turned back to a still life of fruit. "It always changes." Arthur accepted it all: The bananas, spinning and singular and turning brown. The shabby, propped-open window. Felina nudged her hand into his, told him she had an even better idea, that next time they'd use the whole facade, next time would be their *coup de grâce*.

NOTES TO A SHADOWY MAN

VERA HAS SEEN SO MUCH FILM NOIR THAT SOMETIMES, IF SHE squints and holds her breath, she can make daytime dark and indistinct, see the image of a shadowy man on the building across the street. The Illusion is unlike any theater she has ever been to before. Its one small projection room is crowded with worn velvet loveseats and chairs, and sometimes, if she arrives too late, she has to sit pressed close to a stranger.

But almost as much as the theater at night, Vera loves the nearly empty café downstairs during the day. The café reminds her a bit of pictures she saw once of the Crystal Palace in London. The front wall is all windows and fringed drapes, accented by overgrown ferns in cracked pots. In the evening, the café fills with artist types and Vera feels too shy to sit down by herself, but during the day she has read entire books here, the baby asleep beside her.

She's never met another baby like this one, and she's cared for other people's babies since she was twelve, even helped to raise her younger siblings when she was just a child herself. The baby's name is Raffi. He has black hair and dark blue eyes that are so clear they remind her of the glass eyes of a doll. When she picks up Raffi, it's as if she has lifted peace in a soft blue wrap. Raffi is so calm she fears for him.

There are cafés like this in London, or at least in the London of Vera's imagination. She has never been to the city, only to Heathrow for her flight to the States for her first au pair position five years ago. She grew up in a suburb of a suburb of Manchester. Now she lives in Minneapolis. The word still trips on her tongue. At the café, she sits in a summer frock and feels the velvet of the couch against the back of her knees. Raffi has begun to fuss, but even his fussing is quiet. He sucks his bottom lip in and out, stretches two thin fingers and curls them again. Vera strokes her hand over his eyes and forehead and he falls back to sleep. She moves her leg and feels the not unpleasant coldness of copper grommets in the velvet. She will not read today. The book, one of Raffi's mother's paperbacks, does not hold her attention.

She gazes at the movie posters on the wall. The placket beside them says they are lithographs for Polish films that were banned under communism. They are beautiful with their crisp edges and geometrical shapes. She would like a flat someday with artwork like this. She knows exactly what she will wear when she has this flat—gabardine skirt, wide-shouldered silk blouse. She can imagine the man who will live there with her; he will be as suave as the man in the third poster; he will wear a dented hat and a slouchy dark suit.

She carries Raffi into the loo with her. She loves the loo best, for it has never been remodeled. On one side of the room is an ornate vanity table with marquee lights. The vanity is bare except for an antique pearl comb and brush set, and one perfume bottle with a blush-red atomizer. Raffi likes the bright, spotty light. His eyes drift from bulb to bulb and he reaches his arms upward. Vera has spent as long as half an hour here. The first time she stayed so long she worried someone would be waiting outside, or that the barista would say something, but no one even noticed.

She sits at the dressing table and stares at her reflection. She is twenty-four, has ginger hair that curls in the summer heat. Her teeth are spaced too far apart, but she has grown accustomed to her face and daydreams that her shadowy man will tell her he adores her. She does not have clear eyes like Raffi. When she leans close to the mirror, she sees a yellowish tinge. Her irises are a golden brown and her left eye is half-blue. She has never minded the half-blue eye. Has she grown older since coming to America? She cannot tell. She hasn't gotten fat like her mother predicted. And she won't be coming back either, not alone, and not "with a bun in the oven." She squints and looks sidelong into the mirror. The marquee lights spiral and she imagines herself cut by vertical lines of shadow and light. She casts her eyes down to Raffi and pretends he is Bogart's Marlowe. "So you're a private detective," she says, and she repeats the line again, this time in a husky voice. "So you're a private detective. I didn't know they existed, except in books." Raffi coos and she crouches down from her stool and nuzzles into his face. "Silly Vera," she says to him. "Silly, silly, Vera."

She is about to pick up Raffi and leave when she notices a drawer in the vanity. She slides it out slowly, unable to guess what might be inside. But there is nothing inside, just a faded purple lining. Vera is in a café restroom; a baby that is not her own is beside her in a basinet.

Out in the café, she picks up her book and tucks it into

the pocket behind the blue and white checked pram. They call prams "strollers" here. Vera is experienced enough now to know that this stroller is worth nearly her month's pay. Raffi's mother buys only the best. The Fullers have an enormous house, and Mrs. Fuller jokes that she has paid for it with her blood, sweat, and boredom. She is a corporate tax lawyer and works long hours and often comes home after Raffi is already in bed. Vera moved in with the Fullers while Mrs. Fuller was still pregnant, and it was Mrs. Fuller who took her to her first film at The Illusion, a silent one called *The Sealed Room*. Mrs. Fuller shouted and booed with the audience when the evil king sealed up the queen and her lover in her secret room. She grabbed Vera's knee and whispered to her that she wouldn't mind a sealed room of her own, just for a day or two. Vera didn't know what to say, so she said nothing at all, and shook her head when Mrs. Fuller passed her popcorn and Red Vines even though Vera wanted to devour them. Later, over tea in the café, Mrs. Fuller took Vera's hand and told her she needn't be so polite. "You're so young," she said. "Live a little, my god." Now Mrs. Fuller doubts that any young woman could go to the movies so often. She looks at Vera like she's one of her clients, like Vera has something to hide.

Vera pushes the stroller ten blocks, from the rougher neighborhood of the café into the quiet lakeside community where she lives, before she decides she will write a note and place it in the dressing table drawer. She does not know what she will write in the note, but the secrecy of her plan excites her and all evening she annoys Mrs. Fuller with her discreet smile, her scattered attention. "Hello. Earth to Vera," Mrs. Fuller says, during dinner. Later that evening, Vera overhears Mrs. Fuller tell Mr. Fuller that Vera has been acting strange. "Eight months," she says. "Eight months and not even one friend. She still won't call me Paula. Mrs. Fuller. Gives me the chills."

But Vera has made a few friends. On Wednesdays, she visits with the cleaning woman, Rose, and sometimes in the neighborhood park she meets another au pair, a Canadian named Maribeth who has four children in her charge and is always in trouble for the mess they make. The last time Vera saw Maribeth she looked as if she had aged ten years. She always asks Vera to buy her chocolates when Vera goes to shows or out on walks, and when Vera brings them to her, Maribeth does not ask her inside, only whispers "thank you" and quietly closes the door.

Vera fills the plastic tub for Raffi and soaps him up. He doesn't like water and shudders when she pours a handful of suds over his belly. Months ago she removed his shriveled umbilical cord and put it into a plastic envelope in his baby book. She is not sure if Americans follow this practice or if Mrs. Fuller will appreciate it. It occurs to Vera that a navel is really a scar and she rubs her own and wishes she could remember what it was like to be so connected to her own mother. She likes to tickle Raffi there. In the last few months he has fattened up, and the rolls under his knees make her laugh. "You chunky little panda," she calls him and he splays his tiny fingers; he gurgles and blows bubbles. She lifts him from the tub and dries his legs. His face squeezes into a grimace and turns red. He should howl any minute, but he breaks into smile and Vera presses him to her chest. He is wet and fat and squishy, and she buries her nose in his wet skin.

All morning it has thundered. On her way out, Mrs. Fuller tells Vera not to take Raffi outside today, but Vera only hears "… don't forget to unload the dishwasher." In her head, she has written her note. She steals into Mrs. Fuller's study and finds some ivory notepaper with matching envelopes. The paper has the faint smell of vanilla and a watermark that Vera holds to the light. She ruins two pages using the wrong pen, but then finds the perfect thin fountain pen with black, almost purple ink. Her handwriting has never looked so fluid, but she has mixed printed letters in with cursive. Without lines, her words slant downward like they are diving off the page, and she can almost see them, her letters in black bathing suits slipping off the edge. She crumples the paper and hides it in a pocket to toss out in a stranger's rubbish during her walk, then she finds a piece of lined paper, puts it under the good notepaper and begins again.

Raffi is crying. It must be the weather. She bounces him on her knee. She gives him more milk, waits an hour and changes him again. She doesn't want to forget where she left off on the letter. "Shh…. Be good now. We'll go to the café. You like the café."

It is still raining, but not unlike an English rain. Where she comes from people go out in worse weather. She will put the top up on the pram. She will swaddle Raffi with extra blankets. She puts the note in the inside pocket of her raincoat. She has fastened a gold seal on the back and tied it with a magenta ribbon from Mrs. Fuller's gift-wrapping box.

Bobbly, bobbly, bobbly go the wheels of the stroller. She bumps it over potholes and cracks, through puddles. The clouds have billowed in darker. The sky rumbles. The drops are larger now and hammer the stroller hood. Raffi likes to be strolled. He is singing to himself. Vera opens her umbrella and holds it over the stroller, although there is no need. It is a tented room, the stroller, and Raffi is snug.

The café is busy today. Several people stand in a queue for coffee, and at one of the tables three German men drink espresso and discuss film. She can make out that word, "film," but little else. They look as if they have visited the same barber, and she imagines they smell of the same shaving lotion. They do not take notice of Vera or the baby. She waits at the counter for her coffee. "Quite the weather," she says to the barista. She feels almost loquacious. The note is pressed inside her coat like a conversation and goads her on. "Coffee and steamed milk?" the barista asks. "Yes, please," she answers. She fancies herself almost American now, drinking coffee instead of tea. "It's coming down in buckets," she says. The barista only nods. Vera wants to tell her about the strange gold cast to the sky, how for a few minutes the raindrops turned to prisms and everything shimmered.

She takes her coffee to the velvet couch and sits. The German men leave their cups on the table and stand around talking. She thinks of Bogart and Bacall, of the time they were all held hostage during a storm in *Key Largo*. She wishes the Midwest had hurricanes and they would all have to huddle together. She would play a concerned, beautiful mother, and the barista could be a tired vamp. She watches the barista clear the table and try to talk to the men in broken German. She has short bleached blond hair and a pierced eyebrow. The men flirt with her. Vera grins at the girl and the men. She stands and lifts Raffi out of the stroller. He is cold and sweaty. His clear eyes look even more like glass. She bounces him on her knee, but he does not smile. He starts to cry. A middle-aged woman in a raincoat scowls at her as she walks to the counter to order. The German men saunter out of the café and the barista looks over at Vera. "You need a cracker or something?"

"No," Vera says. "He's never like this. He'll be fine." She holds Raffi against her shoulder, feels warm drool on her neck. More people rush in and line up behind the counter. Two women go into the bathroom together to towel off from the rain. One whispers to the other, a secret Vera cannot overhear. Raffi will not stop crying. Something is not right. The women do not come out of the bathroom. Are they sitting at the vanity? Are they brushing their hair? She waits a few more minutes, and by then it seems as if everyone in the café is staring. The woman in the raincoat purses her lips as she sits down at a table with her coffee. Vera carries Raffi outside under the pitched roof. "Look, look at the rain," she whispers.

She sings "Itsy Bitsy Spider." A man walks from across the parking lot to the café. He takes long strides, jumps almost, as if he will stay dry that way. He reminds Vera of a cat, his legs are thin and graceful in his oversized trousers, his shoulders relaxed. He pauses by the door and takes a peek at Raffi. Most assume she is his mother, and she likes to play along. If she tells them she is the nanny, they go away, even twitch their mouths in disdain.

"Better take him inside," says the man. "It's not fit for vegetable or beast out here."

Vera rocks Raffi back and forth. She wonders what Lauren Bacall would say. Something clever and brash, no doubt. With a cool half-smile, she'd tell the man to mind his own business, to get lost. "We won't melt," Vera says. It's not clever, but she is still surprised. Her cheeks burn and she hides her face in Raffi, whispers, "shh…"

"Really, bring the little wailer inside," the man says. "Clear the place out for me." He gives her a silly grin and ducks inside. She turns and watches his silhouette through the window.

Raffi has quieted. No, he has cried himself to sleep. She must get him home. She feels this now in her gut. Her note will have to wait.

But the man is sitting down on the couch beside the pram, and she makes herself sit down too, her breath quaking in her chest, Raffi heavy in her arms. Why is it babies are always so much heavier asleep? The man lowers his newspaper and asks her about Raffi. She tells him she is only watching the child for a few hours for a friend. She only lies a little and the man doesn't leave. He is handsome in a roguish way. He has short whiskers and there are two bare spots at either side of his lips. There is something old-fashioned about him, about the way he crosses his legs, the way he wears his cap so it casts a shadow over his face.

"You have two different colored eyes," he says, and the older woman sitting at the table looks over.

Vera doesn't say anything. Usually, people notice her eyes, but then look away.

"How unusual," he says and she believes that he is quite taken.

The man wants to hear all about England. "I've never been," he says. She tells him she grew up in Manchester, which is almost the truth. She tells him about the factories there, how hip the city has become in recent years. The woman at the table looks at her again. She reminds Vera of her mother in her drab raincoat, her downturned lips. The man thinks it is ironic that so many industrial cities that could never afford to tear down their warehouses are now art centers. "What was that dance place that was so popular in the 90s, you know, the electronica place?"

"The Hacienda," she says. The club closed down when she was just a baby. She wishes she could have danced there. She tells him about raves in huge warehouses she never went to, about an art exhibit she heard about from Mrs. Fuller. She doesn't tell him that she did not go to university, or that she became an au pair at nineteen.

"What a fascinating life you've led," the man says. He uncrosses his legs and then lounges back into the couch, his jacket slouched about his shoulders, a lazy smirk on his face. He seems both nervous and at ease. He looks at her, and then around the room. She has never made a man nervous before.

Raffi's eyes open and he starts to cry just a bit. She rocks him gently. He tenses his arms and legs, and reddens. She presses him against her shoulder, but she can feel his stomach begin to quake.

"Excuse me," she says. "I'd better get him back."

The man holds out his arms. "Here, let me." How soothing his voice is. He stands and bends down and picks up Raffi like he has held lots of babies before. He tucks the blanket under Raffi's chin. "Cute little fellow," he says. He eases back into the couch and soon Raffi falls back to sleep.

The note inside her pocket has brought her this sudden luck. She can feel its gold seal emitting an aura about her. The others notice it too, even the barista, who has warmed her milk and coffee, although Vera never asked. Even the woman at the table tips her head to listen.

"And what about you?" she asks. "Did you grow up here?"

"Yes and no," says the man. "So what's the little guy's name?"

"Raffi." She stands up and glances at the bathroom. "Pardon me," she says to the man. She must put her note in the drawer.

"I'll just be a minute," she says, reaching for the baby, who has wrapped his fingers around the man's finger. The barista straightens the newspapers on the coffee table and peeks at Raffi. "What a sweetheart," she says, tiptoeing back toward the counter.

Vera places Raffi back in the pram and glances at the man.

"We'll keep an eye on him. Don't worry," he says.

"I'll only be a minute," Vera repeats. She turns and can feel the man stare at her behind. She tries to walk slowly, to not hurry. How handsome he is. How handsome and she has not even asked his name, although he knows hers. Inside the bathroom, she presses against the door, pushes the lock in and breathes. To think she almost stayed at home!

She sits down at the dressing table. She picks up the pearl-handled brush and runs it against her hair, careful not to make it frizz. Her hair has turned into a curled mess from the rain and a long tendril springs from the top of her head. She is beautiful. She sees it now. She has one eye that is unlike the other. So unusual. Her lips are lush, not so severe as her face. She takes the note from her pocket. The ribbon has gotten wet and stained the paper pink. She presses the paper to her nose, not so much like vanilla now. It smells like her; it smells like rain. She opens the top drawer. She tucks the note to the very back, where the lining is still pristine, imagines that everything one puts into the drawer magically finds its object.

How funny and secret she is. She must move out into the world, not converse with a drawer. She sees now that she has imagined her secret correspondent as her shadowy man, the one she would meet someday. She imagined he would find the note days or years from now and learn everything about her, all her desires and dreams, how she came to America, how an uncle once took her to the zoo when she was a child, all by herself, without her sisters or her brothers, how he bought her a double ice cream cone and they sat in front of the jaguar cage, watching it stalk back and forth, how she told her uncle she was going to be an American movie star and learn to move just like that, how her uncle told her mother, and her mother began to call her Little-

Miss-Thinks-She's-a-Movie-Star.

And, there *is* a man outside, and he might take her out, or perhaps meet her at the café again. Her life will begin. It will begin. She stands up and attempts to flatten the creases that have dried into her skirt. She opens the door. She sees the empty velvet couch. She sees her cup and the carafe of steamed milk on the coffee table. She sees the pram and knows even before she looks that Raffi is not inside.

The man is at the counter talking to the barista. Three women sit chatting at a table by the front window. Outside it is pouring again.

"Excuse me," Vera calls. Her voice barely rasps from her throat. She stands over the empty pram. Her ankles are jelly. "My baby," she says.

The barista stops wiping the counter. She mirrors back the shock in Vera's face. The man turns. He runs out the door. Vera can see him through the window, in front of the café turning in every direction, pulling a cell phone from his pocket. The rain comes down in sheaves. The barista runs outside too. The women turn to look at Vera, to look outside.

"That woman," Vera says, remembering the lady in the raincoat. Where she was sitting is a full cup of coffee, an untouched biscuit on a plate. "Did you see her leave?"

One of the women says, "Here, come and sit down. Who can we call for you?" She must be a mother because she has that stricken look that mothers get when any baby has been lost. She leads Vera to a chair. Vera grips the wood and sees the café in black and white, in shadows and slats of dizzying light. "It's going to be all right," the woman says. "They'll find your baby. They'll put out an alert."

Vera rushes out the door, past the man and the barista who have ducked under the awning. The man yells, "Wait. I called the police," but Vera keeps running. She circles the block, looking for the woman, trying to recall her face, but only remembering her shapeless coat. The rain has stopped. The sun is out. She trips on the broken sidewalk. She passes a boarded-up pawnshop and an empty lot. She turns around and walks back towards the café and then down another street. A police car stops and an officer gets out and coaxes her into the front seat. "I only left him for a minute," she says, but she can tell by the way he looks at her that he thinks she's one of them, those bad nannies who leave their children alone or shake them to death.

How much like Northern England the Midwest looks from the plane with its dull brown and bright green squares. Only six weeks have passed, but Vera feels a decade older. She has gotten a window seat, although she requested the aisle. Up, up, they go. The businessman next to her clutches both arms of his chair and there is nowhere for Vera to put her hands. She holds them in her lap. She feels her stomach loop. Clouds, layers of clouds, as if the sky were made of sheets of rice paper, gradually becoming more opaque. Vera begins to relax. So many questions. One detective after another, family friends, Mr. Fuller's mother. The Fullers weathered Vera's presence while they canvassed the city with flyers and waited by the phone. They would not allow her to leave. Then Mrs. Fuller crept into Vera's room in the middle of the night and sat at the edge of her bed. In her fist, she clutched a crumpled draft of the note from the pocket of Vera's raincoat. The police had found the original in the café vanity drawer. "If you had something to do with this Vera..." Mrs. Fuller's voice trembled. She tugged the covers off Vera and Vera lay very still. Mrs. Fuller pulled her up by the shoulders and shook her. "If you planned this, so help me God." Then Mr. Fuller came and pulled Mrs. Fuller away. Vera heard the door to their room close. Mrs. Fuller did not leave their room after that. A few weeks later Mr. Fuller bought Vera a plane ticket home. "Don't think this is over," he told her as she rolled her bags out to the cab.

She peers out the plane window again. They are high above the clouds now, the sky an unnatural blue, the clouds below rippled like dunes. Look, Raffi, she says in her mind.

She feels a tug in her navel, a string to the ground. He is down there somewhere, and he will come home. She is certain because she left him a letter in the café powder room, pressed in an envelope with the umbilical cord from his baby book. A last note, on her way to the airport. It was so difficult to write it in secret, to keep it from the Fullers. Everything one puts into the drawer magically finds its object. She knows this. She has seen it happen. In the letter, she has written their last day backwards, hers and Raffi's, from the moment just before she put him in the stranger's arms to the moment he stretched his arms out to her from his crib that rainy morning. *Be well, Raffi*, she has written, in pages and pages, over and over again. *Be well, Raffi. Come home.*

BOYS ON A VERANDA

HE HAD NEVER PAID ATTENTION TO THE WOMAN ACROSS the way before. Now he caught himself holding his breath as he watched her, his tea turning cold. Their brownstones were so close together he could peek through his curtains into her dining room. She must have been about his daughter's age, in her mid-thirties. She rarely had visitors. Instead of sitting down for a simple bowl of soup or salad as he usually did in the evenings, the woman set the table each night and lit a candle. Then she brought out a silver platter stacked with what he discovered were picture postcards.

She separated the cards into stacks, lifting them one at a time and gazing at the pictures or bringing them to her nose. From what he could tell the backs of the cards were blank. When she finally found a satisfactory one, she placed it on her plate. She ripped tiny pieces from the corners as one might tear crumbs from bread. She placed them in her mouth one at a time, closed her eyes and chewed.

He considered knocking on her door. It would be easy enough to discover her apartment number and get into the building. But he was retired and must stop thinking like a psychiatrist, and besides, what pretense would he use? He simply missed his daughter. His story would shock the woman across the way, or encourage pity, and he didn't want that. Three illnesses in less than two years. His wife given just six months. She refused chemo. And then their daughter. It was an impossibility, but she too was diagnosed, and within months of her mother's death she was gone as well.

It was all a sad joke. When he felt the lump in his neck, he laughed out loud. No one would believe this in a movie. He didn't refuse treatment. He went through it all, accepted the volunteers' rides back and forth from the clinic, the deliveries of groceries and medications. He had lost his hair years earlier, and unlike his wife and daughter invited no looks of recognition at what he endured.

His appetite had returned, but everything had a chemical flavor. When he watched the woman across the way, his mouth watered and he drank his tea to wash the bitter taste from his tongue. He was sixty-eight and in otherwise good health. He had sold his practice, and now met friends for coffee or took walks along the lakeshore. He was not one to travel, though his wife had begged him for years to attend more conferences and take her with him. She and their daughter traveled together—Paris, Crete, Maui, Buenos Aires. By the time they decided to travel a last time, to Venice, they had given up on him and didn't even ask him to come along.

Books no longer interested him, but he tried to read a novel. His apartment was too silent, even with the cat and the television. As he watched the woman across the way, he remembered the postcard his daughter sent during that trip—an impressionist painting of three boys on a veranda overlooking the sea, in blues, pinks, reds, and yellows. The boys held a toy boat. There were sailboats in the bay behind them. The painting was by a Finnish artist and had nothing to do with Venice, though the inscription was in Italian. He remembered thinking about this, how it wouldn't have seemed strange to him that it was Finnish if it had come from an American museum with an English inscription.

One evening when the woman set her table, he set his own. He boiled water for tea. It was good tea, from a canister he found outside his building with a note that said *free* and *for your happiness*. His next-door neighbor told him he was suicidal to drink it. "What if it's poisoned?" But he took the gift as a sign that things would get easier. He watched the bundle of tea blossom in his cup. He washed a place setting from his wife's china set and found a half-burned candle in a drawer in the kitchen. He fetched the postcard from his daughter and placed it in a serving bowl. The cat hopped onto the table to watch.

At night, it was more difficult to observe the woman without being seen. He opened the lacy curtains a few inches. It was almost like they were having dinner together. He thought she caught him staring, but she was gazing into space. He read the back of his postcard: *Well, we made it. See, Dad? No nosedive into the ocean. We're going to eat our way through the city. Mom said to tell you not to take every meal at the diner, and also she's going to have a brief affair with a gondolier. Ha ha!*

He tore off a corner. In everything that medicinal flavor, but it was comforting to know that in this case it was due to dyes in the paper. He closed his eyes and tried to remember the smell of his daughter's hair when she was two. He smelled salt water and sea air instead, a psychosomatic response.

He turned the postcard over and left the table. The woman across the way practiced a ritual of loneliness, and he had wanted such a ritual too. He found it amusing that he was like so many of his patients, that he could feel like an orphan at his age. He went for a walk, past the park where the old played *Bocce*. He refused to think of himself that way, as one of the old. He walked all over the city and when he returned home his cat wrapped herself around his leg and begged to be fed.

Unlike her, he could no longer bear routine.

He'd have to find someone to look after her when he went away.

He had a phobia of flying. He had denied this to his daughter and his wife, had told them that travel was unnecessary once you realized that every place was essentially the same. He pretended a Buddhist sensibility. They had never believed him. Now he bought a ticket to Venice.

He leased his apartment to a conscientious intern on rotations at the hospital and asked him to take care of the cat. He tucked the postcard into his pocket and packed a bag with a few changes of clothing. He'd stay just long enough to gaze at the sea and put his feet in the water. And he wasn't afraid this time. He felt none of the familiar lack of air and space in the plane, nor the downward pull of gravity. When the flight attendant delivered a plastic plate with chicken and half-frozen carrots, he was surprised that there was, for the first time in months, no aftertaste.

At the airport in Venice, he chose the poorest most disreputable looking taxi driver and careened through the city to the very hotel where his wife and daughter had stayed. He didn't know what room they had booked. His was on the second floor above the street, away from the canals and the ocean. That evening, he rode a gondola and dined out on shellfish though his guidebook warned against it.

In his suitcase he had packed a rope and instructions for his body. He would spend one more day and one more night, and then he would step off a chair and it would be over. He liked the simplicity of his plan. At a café, he ordered a bottle of Chianti and sipped it at an outside table. A jewelry vendor with large jowls and a neck laden with gold joined him. "A pretty necklace for the wife?"

He bought the cheap, gold necklace and put it into his pocket with the postcard. He offered a glass of wine to the vendor and listened as the man spoke in fragmented English about the many places the psychiatrist should visit. Everything acquired a pretty blur. Under the table, the psychiatrist pulled out the postcard and tore off a bit and popped it into his mouth like a pill, washing it down with more wine. Down the street a woman played guitar and sang the blues. She was American, not Italian. Her voice was ordinary, but a crowd gathered nonetheless. On his way out of the restaurant, he dropped the necklace into her case.

In the morning, it rained. He took his coffee in his room before the open balcony and threw bread to the pigeons. Then he went down to the lobby to wait for his ride to the beach. By the time he reached the sea, the rain had stopped, though the sky remained muddy and not at all like the sky on the postcard. He took off his loafers and his socks and waded into the water near a group of teenagers bodysurfing. A gull circled and dove. He sat down and let the waves soak his trousers and watched sand and water pour through his fingers. The last time he had waded into the ocean was during a semester-long residency in California. He had a lover there, an Irish colleague with perpetually sunburnt skin, and they sometimes spent weekends rollicking at the sea. He eventually came clean to his wife about the affair. It had taken fifteen years for her to forgive him, and he sometimes wondered if this was the reason she hadn't asked him to come along to Venice.

The teenagers were laughing and when he looked over, one was mimicking him by sitting in the waves and crying into his hands, which sounded especially pathetic in an Italian accent. The psychiatrist stood and walked out of the water. Just you wait, he thought. Your time will come too. His anger surprised him, but so did his embarrassment as he pulled himself from the waves with his pants sticking to his legs. He had lost all sense of propriety, and a part of him was proud for he had always concerned himself too much with the opinions of others.

When he reached his hotel room, he pulled out what was left of the wrinkled, waterlogged postcard—a distant bay, a few sailboats, the red of a boy's beret. He tore off a piece and was about to place it in his mouth when he remembered the patient who had to be restrained in her bed to keep her from eating the bed railings and even her own hands. He hadn't truly understood her until then.

He turned the paper scrap over and read the words, *tomorrow Ferrara*. He couldn't recall his wife or daughter mentioning anything about a town called Ferrara.

That evening on his veranda, he listened to music from a dance club down the street and toyed with the rope in his hands. He couldn't find a sturdy place in the room to hang it from, and he wouldn't subject the tourists below to such a horrific display. He made a noose and tied the rope to the shower bar. He moved the chair underneath and climbed onto it. When he stepped off, he found that he had tied the rope too long. It hung slack around his neck. He adjusted the length and tried again. This time the bar ripped from its mounting. He catapulted forward and hit his head on the sink, and imagined the *hotelier* discovering him collapsed and unconscious next to the toilet. A tourist from Chicago. A psychiatrist no less. *Tied a rope to a spring-loaded shower bar.* He thought of the many stories he had heard over the years, from patients and doctors alike. If he had succeeded there might have been an autopsy. *Belly full of linguini with clams. Cancer survivor.* Who would they have contacted for next of kin? He could fill volumes with stories of botched suicides and unclaimed bodies, some so ridiculous you couldn't help but laugh.

He wiped the blood from his forehead and went to bed.

In the morning, he turned over the stained pillow. Then he looked up Ferrara in his guidebook. It was just a short train ride away. He packed his things. He coiled the rope and stuffed it into the wastebasket under the desk.

At the train station gift shop, he purchased some envelopes and notecards, along with a black and white postcard of a girl waiting for a train with a schnauzer on her lap. Then he stood before the railway map and remembered how his daughter had poured over maps at the dining table when she was a child, tracing her finger from one town to the next just to hear herself pronounce foreign cities. He read aloud from the map now and heard her voice: *Ferrara. Malabergo. San Giorgio di Piano.* He sat down on a bench and scribbled a note to his renter to deliver to the woman in the apartment across the way. When he was tired of traveling, he would return home and visit her. *Tell her I will send others,* he wrote. *Tell her this is for her happiness. Tell her the next one will be full of color with something good to eat.*

EDITH UNDER THE STREETLIGHT

WHEN SANDRA COULDN'T COME UP WITH HER RENT that summer, she turned to Edith who lived down the hall. Edith, who didn't have a friend in the world, who stopped by Sandra's apartment several times a day to complain about the noisy girls who lived in the apartment between them. She was so gaunt and swollen-jointed, so narrow in the face, she reminded Sandra of a wigged praying mantis. It wasn't Edith's fault that she had gotten old. And, it wasn't Sandra's fault that her work on the survival instincts of the *Melanoplus bivittatus*, a two-striped grasshopper with an elaborate hatch cycle, was still going nowhere. The university had refused her last request for an extension. She had lost her research space. Now she'd be lucky to find a job as a lab assistant.

She lied and told Edith she had lost her funding due to budget cuts. "I'll pay you back. I promise."

Edith was overly pleased. She clasped her bony hands together and said, "Don't you worry your smart little head. We gals got to stick together."

She was at Sandra's door again now, the second time that afternoon, with Danny Boy, her drooling, half-blind basset hound. Edith's hair sprang from the top of her head, her eyes bulged, and she inched too close. "Those nitwits are at it again," she said. "The Kadars moved out this morning, and you know what that means.

Those girls will bring in more of their bubblehead friends."

She peeked into Sandra's apartment. "I see they drove your roommate out."

"She's just away for the summer," Sandra said, though her roommate was doing fieldwork in East Africa and was moving out in the fall.

Edith handed Sandra a typed paper and winked. "This one is particularly brilliant. They won't ignore us now, kiddo."

It was a new petition. Edith had been writing them ever since the girls moved in next door. Their landlord would laugh when he saw the antiquated typescript. It didn't help that one of the girls was his niece, that the police never issued more than a verbal warning to them about the noise.

At the top of the page, Edith had written what appeared to be a manifesto. She used the words *whereas* and *therefore*, and *community* and *solidarity*, and even included references to Thomas Paine and Simone de Beauvoir.

When she noticed Sandra staring at the empty lines below her own signature, Edith said, "We'll forge the rest."

She handed Sandra a pen. "Hear that? Sleeping like babies, after that racket last night. What we need is an air horn."

Sandra pressed the petition against the wall and signed. "I've been applying for jobs," she said. "I should be able to pay you back soon."

But she hadn't applied for jobs. She had only browsed employment sites on her laptop while watching all-night marathons of *Law & Order* and *CSI*.

At that time of night, with the walls throbbing from her neighbors' music and the balmy air filtering in through her open balcony, her senses were inordinately acute. She began to notice a disturbing pattern of ghastly and beautiful female corpses on television, many like her next-door neighbors—flirty, scantily clad college girls murdered in back alleys and stairwells.

She jotted notes in a lab book, a force of habit. Sometimes she even imagined the building as a Skinner box and took notes on all the tenants.

Now she tallied stiletto heels, fishnet stockings, tattoos, miniature dogs. She counted private-school runaways and heroin-addicted hookers, bored housewives and ambitious career women.

The youngest and most beautiful were often discarded in dank subways or landfills, or tossed under viaducts. Nearly all of them were in states of undress, their skirts hiked to their hips, their blouses torn.

She had recorded hours of programs, and she fast-forwarded and paused at crime scene stills. The victims weren't actors so much as models. They were like fresh fruit masquerading as rotten fruit in a still life—no matter how much make-up they wore they pulsated with life.

Some pygmy grasshoppers turned the color of stalks and mud and feigned death to survive. In her living room closet were boxes of lab books detailing the demise of thousands of two-striped hoppers. All that work. All those lives.

It had never bothered her until the last annual National Entomological Society meeting, where she listened to two rock star academics deliver a lecture on the "vibrational communiqués of anthropods, from the miniscule aphid to the flinty treehopper." They called themselves acoustic ecologists and used laser vibrometers to record hundreds of types of insects thumping and clicking and making sounds for which verbs had yet to be invented.

The lacewing sounded like live power lines, phantom midges like a score to a Hitchcock film. For their grand finale, the men played all the sounds at once. The audience swooned. Sandra resisted an urge to cry out when she detected the sound of the Two-striped in all that noise.

Still she had returned to the lab and measured femur and body length. She had catalogued variations in color patterns. She had subjected her samples, mostly nymphs and mature females, to predators and extreme temperature changes, coercing them into winter diapause.

Now she contemplated the feigned death of actors on screen.

The less skilled sometimes let their chests heave or their lashes flitter or their nostrils flare. It was hardest for the children to pull off, and sometimes Sandra detected the urge to giggle on their lips. While she watched, she never felt fear. Fear didn't arrive until she went to bed and remembered the evening news, the woman found dead in the trunk of her car, the man who had been breaking into apartments all over the city.

One night, Sandra heard a woman's horrifying, piercing scream coming from outside and without thinking she rushed down the stairs. But when she reached the street, it was all three girls from next door, drunk and screaming for sheer pleasure.

They were still laughing when she reached her apartment and heard them from her balcony. *Did you see her pajamas? What a wack job. No wonder she spends so much time with that creepy old lady.*

She closed the door and sunk down in front of the TV with the sound turned off. The girls were in the hallway now, squealing and slamming into the walls. It sounded like a game of human bowling. She heard Edith then, threatening to call the police. "Your neighbor is trying to earn her doctorate," she said. "She needs her sleep."

For some reason, this made the girls howl with laughter. Sandra wanted to go and thank Edith for standing up for her, for being the only person even interested in her work. She had a specimen jar beside her. Inside was a young female with a deformed forewing that she had gradually frozen to death during one of her last experiments. She picked up the jar and opened the lid, and nudged it with her finger. It had never come out of diapause. She had named her Calliope.

"I'm not like Edith," she told herself. "I have friends. They're just in other cities." She set the jar down on the coffee table. The girls were back inside their own apartment and the walls reverberated with their music. They were dancing now and shouting. And then someone fell and glass broke, and there was a pause and then more hysterical laughter.

On the television, a young woman opened her bathroom

door to find her slain roommate in the bathtub, her bloody arm hanging over the side. Sandra paused on the image. She fetched her laptop and looked up recipes for fake blood. She was inspired—it was all she could do to not share her plan with Edith.

That next night, she waited on her balcony for the girls to go out. Down below, Edith walked Danny Boy one last time before retiring for the night. She stood under the streetlight and waved to Sandra, and Sandra waved back.

Next door, the girls shouted back and forth as they dressed for the clubs. They were so predictable, leaving by eight or nine, returning just after bar time. Their balcony door was open, and Sandra could hear their cell phones ringing and the shower running and their hair dryers blasting. The blondest of the three, Nicole, was a marketing major who spent all afternoon on the balcony talking on the phone. The athletic one—Sandra could never remember her name—was always dieting. Once Sandra spied her dumping a bowl of chocolate pudding from the balcony, just missing Edith. And the third roommate, Zoe, barely tolerated her roommates and played bass in a band.

Nicole brought a bottle of tequila to the balcony and poured herself a shot. Her musky perfume wafted over to Sandra, and Sandra covered her nose.

"Don't you have anything better to do?" Nicole said. "Like I know you're always watching us." She lit a cigarette and yelled for Katie to come outside. So the athletic roommate's name was Katie?

Nicole stared at Sandra. "Do you mind?"

"I can't help it if our balconies are so close," Sandra said. It was true, without much effort she could climb over the railing and reach for the shot Nicole had just poured.

"Why don't you get your own life? Stop calling the landlord on us."

Before Sandra could respond, Nicole went back inside.

A few minutes later, all three girls tromped down the stairs and out to Nicole's jeep, and Sandra hurried inside. She poured the corn syrup blood she made that afternoon into a baggie and wound her hair in hot rollers. She dug into her sock drawer for the pair of fishnet stockings she once wore to a Halloween party.

It had been too long since she had felt this energized, this focused.

She raided her roommate's closet for her red, low-cut dress and her spiked heels. She rummaged through her bathroom drawer for red lipstick that she slicked on and then smeared down her chin. Under her eyes and in streaks around her neck, she daubed blue and charcoal eye shadow.

When she looked in the mirror, she saw a battered and bruised, and not unattractive, woman looking back at her.

She went to the balcony to calm herself.

The neighborhood held that temporary pre-bar-time stillness. She leaned back on the railing and looked down at Calliope in her jar on the table. Her faded taupe appeared iridescent green and alive. Sandra took off the lid for a better look, but Calliope lay on her side, brittle and still.

It must have been the streetlight playing tricks.

At one-thirty, she stole into the hallway with her baggie

of blood. She waited, listening, for the downstairs door to open, for footsteps and the girls' voices. She arranged herself over the landing with her dress hiked, one shoe dangling off her left foot, her other leg folded beneath her. She bit a hole in the bag and poured the blood over her chest, smearing it in her hair and across her neck and tucking the empty bag into her bra. When she heard the downstairs door, she put her head down.

The carpet smelled of mildew and deodorizer. If she had thought of it earlier, she would have dropped some curious object, perhaps a Russian coin or a Yoruban fertility doll. She slowed her breathing and practiced a taken-too-soon-by-a-violent-John look.

Moments later, she heard a door open. Danny Boy pattered into the hallway, followed by Edith. Edith never left her apartment after midnight. Sandra stiffened and tried not to breath. Her heart palpitated.

She had left the door to her apartment open, Mahler's ominous last symphony playing on repeat to add verisimilitude to the scene. Her blood beat in her wrists and in her neck. She quelled a sudden twitch in her upper lip.

Danny Boy whined and jerked at his leash. He nosed in Sandra's direction.

Edith's voice was a raw whisper. "My god," she said.

Then, "Are you all right? I'm calling for help."

After Edith rushed to her apartment, pulling Danny Boy after her, Sandra shot up. She held her hands over her dripping neck and ran into her apartment, shutting the door quietly. She turned off the stereo, undressed and stuffed her clothes under her roommate's bed. She rinsed herself in the shower and put on her bathrobe and turned on the television, mortified by the madness of her failed plan.

Two police cars pulled up outside. Blue and red lights spun on Sandra's walls. Then she watched as the girls piled out of Nicole's jeep. Sandra peered out her door as officers clamored up the stairs and into the hallway. The girls ran behind them shouting, "What's going on? What happened?"

Then Edith appeared from her apartment. It was a shock to see her in her natty sweatpants, her face blanched of makeup, her nearly bald eyebrows arched in horror. Danny Boy bellowed from behind her door. Edith pointed towards the stairs. Then she saw Sandra and her eyes narrowed. She tilted her head to stare. "She was right over there," she said. "No, above the first landing. Over there."

The officers shone their flashlights over the stairs and windows. Edith looked at Sandra's apartment door and then at Sandra. "It was *you*," she said. "Your door was open." She stepped closer. She touched a damp lock of Sandra's hair. "Yes, it *was* you."

Sandra glanced from Edith to the officers. They looked nothing like TV detectives. One officer had freckles and a thin, slicked-back ponytail, and her Billy club reached nearly to her knees. Her partner was tall and awkward. He shifted his weight from leg to leg as a third officer bounced a flashlight from floor to wall to window. Even with the poor lighting, even with the ornate pattern of the rug, Sandra noticed a few dark spots, but not the officers, and not even Edith, who was speechless now, still staring at Sandra.

"Everyone back inside," the policewoman said. "*You*," she said to Edith. "You stay here."

Sandra retreated into her apartment and scrubbed the counters and the stove again. She took the baggie from the trash under the sink and buried it under her potted fig, and then she went to the window and watched the first squad car pull away.

When the remaining policeman knocked on her door to ask if she had heard anything strange that evening, Sandra told him she had been watching television, perhaps a little too loudly. He lowered his voice and said, "So you didn't leave your door open tonight, Ma'am?"

"Just when I went down to get my laundry."

"And what time was that?"

"About a half hour ago. Should I be worried?"

"Between you and me, I think your neighbor is getting a little senile," he said. Sandra laughed like one of the girls next door. The officer glanced at her loosening robe. "You shouldn't leave your door open like that though," he said. "Never know what might happen."

Over the next few days Sandra stayed inside and drafted an e-mail to her father asking for money, so she could repay Edith. She remembered Calliope and went to the balcony to retrieve her, but the specimen jar was empty. She must have blown out. Sandra searched the deck and found only a few dried leaves.

She tried to revive her interest in police dramas, but now

when she watched she noticed a propensity of victims like Edith—homely recluses subjected to the most undignified of deaths. They died of fright while clutching a cream puff, or were discovered too late, sprawled across kitchen floors in ragged bathrobes with cats milling about.

There were also victims like Sandra—repressed analytical types, murdered in labs by megalomaniac professors or crazed janitors—their horn-rimmed glasses askew, their faces half-erased by chemicals.

The apartment was too silent now. Even the girls next door were unusually quiet. At night, Sandra waited until Edith went to bed before leaving the building.

On one such night, returning well past midnight, she ran into Edith in the hallway. Edith marched towards her, shaking her finger. "That was a nasty little prank," she said. "I'm astounded really. I had you pegged all wrong."

Sandra wanted to apologize, to explain why she had done what she had done, but she didn't fully understand it herself. She held up her hands and backed away. "I don't know what you're talking about. If this is about the money, I'll have it soon."

When she reached her apartment, she gathered her notebooks and threw them into the trash behind the building. She avoided Edith after this, refused to come to her door when Edith knocked, left the building only when Edith was out walking Danny Boy. She stayed at the library until it closed, and then she haunted an all-night café drinking cheap coffee. When she returned, she watched Edith's apartment window until she saw her figure, and only then slipped back inside. More than once

Edith scanned the street from her balcony as if she knew Sandra was out there.

One night, Sandra noticed a second figure in Edith's window, a hulking man crossing back and forth in front of the curtains. She'd never known anyone to visit Edith before.

A few nights later, she returned home to find Edith's windows dark. When she finally risked the downstairs lobby, she discovered Danny Boy, his leash still connected to his collar. She walked him up the stairs, planning to knock on Edith's door and run, but the door was ajar.

She knocked, and no one answered, so she peeked inside and turned on the light. There was evidence of a scuffle, books, pictures hanging askew, vases and lamps toppled and broken.

At first Sandra thought Edith was only retaliating with her own prank, but the air smelled fetid and sweet. Flies buzzed.

"Hello?" Sandra called.

Danny Boy sniffed at an upturned lamp and scurried down the hallway towards the bedroom. Sandra's palms perspired and there was a metallic taste in her mouth. She contemplated turning around and calling the police. She was about to walk to the bedroom when she heard her neighbors' voices outside. She ran into the hallway to find Nicole and Katie.

"You better call the police," Sandra said, and the sound of her own voice frightened her.

Instead they followed Sandra as she tiptoed back into Edith's apartment and down the hallway towards the bedroom where they could hear Danny Boy crying. Nicole clutched the back of Sandra's shirt and Katie cowered behind Nicole, and the three scuttled together as a single organism.

"Stand back," Sandra said, and she pulled away from Nicole to set a lamp upright and turn it on.

Edith was lying face down on the bed. Her filmy nightgown was ripped and bloody, her sheets twisted around a bare, bruised leg. She had dyed her hair bright orange, and a pillow partially covered her head. One thin arm hung over the edge of the mattress, and Danny Boy licked her still hand.

"Is she dead?" Katie whispered.

"I'm not touching her," Nicole said. But then she stepped forward and lifted the pillow. Edith's face was turned to the side, her heavily made-up eyes were wide open, her mouth twisted. Nicole screeched and quick-stepped in place before tearing out of the apartment. Katie ran squealing after her.

Sandra stared at Edith's eyes and nostrils. She tiptoed closer, and just as she touched Edith's soft, cool flesh, Edith shot up from the bed.

Sandra gasped and rushed for the door before stopping and slowly turning around. Edith sat at the edge of her bed, laughing so hard she started coughing and couldn't catch her breath. Tears rolled down her powdered cheeks. Then Sandra noticed the notebooks beside her, *her* notebooks, the ones she had thrown away. She hadn't noticed them until now.

"You're crazy."

"Am I?"

Sandra sank into a chair near the bed. She picked up a pillow from the floor and held it on her lap. "I guess we're even."

"I haven't had that much fun in years," Edith said. "Thrilling. Absolutely thrilling."

"You know they're calling the police?"

Edith ushered Sandra to the door. "Don't you worry about a thing, sweetheart." She had one of Sandra's notebooks in her hand. She opened it to an earmarked page and read aloud: *Edith from 4C. Old. Lonely. Unkempt. Occupation: Apparently none. Walks dog four times a day, never later than eleven P.M. Not worthy of further study.*

"Those are mine."

"Finders keepers," Edith said. "You know what your problem is? Limited imagination. See those flies? Smell that? *Bad ham.* Left it out in the heat for *five days.* Did you see that man the other night? Found him at the market on the corner. Paid him fifty bucks. That's what I call follow through, honey. We're going to shake up this place. Drive them out. Stick with me and you just might learn something."

"I'll have your money tomorrow," she said, but her father had refused to send more.

Sandra turned to walk away, and Edith grabbed her arm. "Forget it," she said. "There are more important things."

After the police left, this time threatening to charge all the women for their repeated false reports and noise violations, the girls next door invited Sandra over for a drink. She sat in their living room listening for movement in the hallway, all too aware of Edith in the next apartment, perhaps with her ear to the wall.

"That woman freaks me out," Katie said. "What a psycho."

"I can't believe she tried to frame us," Nicole said.

Edith had told the police she had simply been rehearsing some performance art when the girls of 4B barged into her apartment, knocking over her things. She hadn't implicated Sandra at all, and she wasn't willing to press charges.

The girls glowed from the shared weirdness of the experience with a woman named *Edith*. Now when Sandra turned the name over on her tongue, it *did* sound decrepit. She wanted to tell them that someday their own names would sound old-fashioned too.

"She probably turns into a bat at night," Zoe said, disappointed at having missed the spectacle. "Or she's got a rocking chair somewhere with her dead husband in it."

Sandra couldn't stop laughing, but this laughter wasn't pleasant. She couldn't regulate her breath. Her hand had trouble gripping the glass.

"She's obsessed with you," Nicole said to Sandra, and Zoe and Katie agreed. They had seen Edith pacing outside Sandra's apartment on more than one occasion and had watched her standing on the sidewalk staring up at her balcony. Why else would Edith not have even mentioned her to the police? And, Katie said, "Remember how she thought she saw Sandra dead out in the hallway that night?" She shuddered. "If I were you, I'd keep my doors locked."

They offered Sandra cookie dough and warm wine, and told her if she ever felt afraid she should come right over. Nicole talked about how funny it was the night Sandra ran outside in her pajamas to save them. They had thought she was just a nerdy weirdo, but she was genuine and brave, like a big sister or an aunt, and they were lucky to have her next door. They sent her home with the remaining wine. "If you need us, just knock on our wall. Like three times or something, so we know it's you."

And they would be quieter too. No more parties during the week, they promised.

When Sandra left that evening, she found a note under her door from Edith requesting she visit 4C for a *postmortem*. Edith would be up late, and Sandra best make herself available. "Liberation is an art," Edith wrote, "one that requires a captive audience." She had just the *milieu* in mind for their next *coup de cadavre*.

Sandra crumpled the note and considered her lack of options. She had to move out, but where would she go? And how would she pay for it?

Not a sound came from the girls' apartment. She stepped onto the balcony. Not a single car passed. The streets were empty. Then she heard shuffling below on the sidewalk. Edith stood under the streetlight with Danny Boy, her hair glowing a brilliant chemical orange, a cloud of gnats and flying insects about her. She caught Sandra's gaze and waved the wave of co-conspirator.

If only Sandra had a friend she could stay with, and a diversion—something unruly enough to allow her to sneak out with a few boxes. Perhaps she could convince the girls next door to throw one more party.

She withdrew into her apartment, locked her front door, and then worried suddenly that Edith, having lived in the building for so many years, might have a key. Sandra had never asked her how she had lived her life before finding herself alone in 4C. Only now did she note how odd Edith's vocabulary was. Her apartment was full of books and strange paintings and figurines. If only Sandra could get inside to retrieve her notebooks. It made no sense, but until she had them back, until she had destroyed them, Edith would have a piece of her, and evidence too.

Downstairs Edith opened the heavy front door and climbed the stairs. Sandra turned off the lights and hunched down on the couch before the open balcony, the slight breeze lifting the drapes. She heard the grunt of the loose railing, Danny Boy tramping behind Edith. After a few minutes, there was a knock at Sandra's door, and then a more persistent pounding. Finally, it stopped. Sandra tried to convince herself that she would not give in. She would not take the wine the girls had given her and try to placate Edith. She would not be at her beck and call. She remained where she was and focused on the rhythm of cicadas outside. She tried to hear crickets and fruit bats and night birds, to discern variations in frequency. She closed her eyes, but each time she caught an individual strain, it vanished into the melody of the swarm.

MITZ'S THEORY
OF EVERYTHING SERIES

It was Mitz who was in Ona's drawings, over and over again. See? That's Mitz lying on a bed, her arms detached at the elbows and reaching up to Ona from the floor. That's Mitz with her narrow hips, and her hair falling out in monstrous, feral clumps. And look, there's Ona. The old Ona. Wholesome Ona. Mitz's Midwestern Apple Pie Girl. Mitz's Peaches and Cream. So tall, her arms reach out of the frame, her breasts balloon to the ceiling. When one grows thin, the other must grow full. It's a law of nature. Symbiotic. Mitz would call it neurotic, codependent.

But where was Mitz now? And why wouldn't she call Ona? Nearly two years as inseparable roommates at the "Harvard of the Midwest," or as Mitz called it, "College for East Coast Fuckups," and not a single phone call or e-mail. Nearly two years together before Ona transferred to a state school, before Mitz dropped out, went AWOL. Even her parents didn't know where she was. Child of science and math camps. Daughter of a Manhattan bank executive and a neurologist. Everyone saw it coming, especially Mitz. "It's the stereotype you fear most that you can't escape," she'd say.

Ona tried to escape. Those first weeks at college, she told herself she wouldn't be like the other Midwesterners—the ones

Mitz impersonated, the ones who worked in the cafeteria, who apologized their way through lecture halls. Clothing was for reinvention and Ona made herself SoHo Boho chic. She razored holes in dresses from Goodwill and wore them over jeans with baubles and beads. She practiced disaffected like Mitz practiced sane.

Now, when Ona walked through her new campus, past its squat modern buildings, she thought she saw her father, his hands thrust in his pockets, a newspaper tucked under his arm. She grew thin from working double shifts at the bookstore café and skipping meals, from staying up all night to draw. When she caught her reflection in a shop window and saw her dress hanging from her bony shoulders, she told herself Mitz was eating somewhere, her hair growing thick.

Ona called Mitz's parents. "Just let me talk to her." She didn't say please. She didn't apologize for not telling them about the food stuffed into Kleenex boxes and thrown into the trash, about Mitz's endless project to discover a theory for all human activity, a theory that as the months passed connected African famines with the changing shape of the earth's core, Navy sonar, aquatic crustaceans, the Monsanto seed bank, and the hypothalamus gland.

Mitz's mother's voice was so calm it bordered on hysterical. "We don't know where she is," she said. "She left the hospital. She isn't using her cell phone or her credit cards. You must know something. Someone she trusted? A friend?"

Ona *was* the friend. There were even rumors they had been

lovers. Mitz had encouraged them. She took Ona's hand when they walked across the quad. She showered Ona with pet names. *Dumpling. My little chick. My big hunk of Wisconsin cheddar.* At night, when Mitz couldn't sleep, she crawled into Ona's bed and asked Ona to tell her stories. She wanted to hear about skating on rivers and Friday night fish fries. Mitz was the only one Ona told about her father, how his exposure to asbestos was both killing him and paying for her education. She dreaded his calls. She couldn't bear his making a joke of everything just to spare her. He never uttered the words *mesothelioma* or *settlement*. "How's life at Harvard?" he'd ask. "You doing us proud?"

"He sounds gallant," Mitz said. "You won't get it, you know. It's not catchy."

But Mitz was catchy. Look, there's Mitz on the vintage Nakishima dining table, an apple between her teeth. There's Ona reaching over with the serving fork. She prefers a leg. The man to her right, with the tall top hat and the banker tie, his arm raised high? That's Mitz's father. "Send it back," he cries. "Give me something with a little meat."

"Disturbing," said the guy behind the easel next to Ona. He whispered to her all through class. "You're supposed to paint what's on the table. It's a *still* life. You're not supposed to improvise."

But look at the broken chair, Ona pointed. Look at the silver platter, the empty pant leg hanging over the edge.

She should have said, it's there, all there, between the objects, rising up. If she had one more hour, she could even resurrect Mitz's parents' ramshackle cottage on Martha's Vineyard. Its chairs with unraveling rush seats, its leather loungers and end tables loaded with modern pottery, Victorian silver, and coffee-stained books and magazines. "We're terrible," Mitz's mother, Simone, had admitted when she caught Ona staring at a glued-together Gambone vase. "There are pieces missing. I can't bring myself to throw it away."

Mitz said, "You wanted to know the difference between old and new money? This is it."

The walls were covered with framed portraits of ancestors and unframed canvases. Mitz's parents had collected art when they were younger. Agnes Martin. Richard Tuttle. Frank Stella. Even an O'Keeffe, the paint cracking from sun and mist. And photographs. Mitz's mother standing knee-deep in the ocean in a long dress, her hair flying. Mitz as a baby, pouring sand into the air. There were no pictures of Mitz as a teenager. "The grim years," Mitz said. "I wasn't pretty then."

Two weeks of blind life-drawings. Ona's instructor stood next to the wooden platform inside their circle of easels. "Eyes on the model, folks." He whacked a yardstick on the metal chair next to Ona. "Up, off the paper. You're not feeling. Feel her mass."

When Ona looked down at her sketch, she saw two misshapen eyes, arms floating, hair unmoored, and only the faintest notion of a torso dripping. So unlike the fleshy model before her. Ona was getting closer. But still she couldn't quite capture Mitz. She couldn't locate her in the body. Mitz was in the voice, the brain, the rooms she inhabited.

After her transfer to the state school, Ona made acquaintances only. She told herself she liked it this way. She pretended she was from far away. When she spoke, she pressed the sound straight through her lips and tried not to bend her vowels. In the end they always guessed. *Chicago? Detroit? Milwaukee?*

"You can take the girl out of Wisconsin," Mitz would say. "But you can't get her to stop saying *holy cow.*"

Mitz had taken Ona out of Wisconsin. That summer on the Vineyard, the two of them working as interns at a magazine called *Sailing Away*, Ona thought it might be that easy, she might just sail into a future of her own making. It would be a new beginning after too many nights partying, after academic probation and her advisor's warning about the permanence of records.

"Let me tell you something about permanent records," Mitz said. "I had a genius test at two. Psych evaluations at four. IQ tests. Rorschach. DSM-IV. Ennea-fucking-gram. Just wait until you meet my parents. They find out you're on probation and you'll be taking a learning-disorder test for dinner."

At *Sailing Away*, Mitz wrote unintelligible twenty-page manifestos and begged the editor to print them. The editor took Mitz off the events beat, sent her to the front desk to do menial tasks. Mitz stuck stamps on the wrong side of envelopes. She put people on hold and forgot them. She left for coffee and returned hours later with plastic bags filled with garbage from the bay.

Ona, on the other hand, was made for magazine work. No

cheese factory, no foundry, no tending bar back home for her. The editor asked her to cover the Taste of the Vineyard festival. "Three hundred words, tops, please."

She shouldn't have brought Mitz.

Eight men and two women ripping apart bushels of crabs, a carnage of shells and flesh and butter.

College Girl Assaults Contestants. Charges Pending.

Mitz's father chose to call it "activism gone awry." He arranged for two weeks of community service doing what Mitz loved best, cleaning the beach, amassing more evidence for her theory of everything.

Those last weeks of break, they woke before dawn to pull crab traps out of the bay from the dock behind the house, to empty them into the water before Mitz's father could check them. Only sometimes a crab would get back in. Crawl right in, even when there wasn't any bait. Mitz called them suicide crabs. She couldn't watch her father lower them into the boiling water. She'd cover her ears. She'd refuse dinner. She believed crabs had a higher intelligence unrecognizable to humans. "You're blind," Simone said to her husband, "if you don't think it's happening all over again."

"You're overreacting," he said. "Mitz is fine." And to Ona, "She hasn't had any trouble at school, has she? You'd tell us if there was anything we should know?"

Sometimes the charcoal jerked sharply, the fingers refused to be polite, a figure's hands turned to claws. Sometimes she scurried into a corner and stared up at a fat, wholesome girl holding a bucket.

"The Crab Lady. I like it. You've got the beginning of a series for your senior thesis," her professor said. "You found a vein."

It was Mitz who had led Ona to her first art class, who hacked into Ona's student account and dropped Calculus I, Theories of Civil Society, and Intermediate Mandarin to enroll her in Two-Dimensional Design, Physics for Poets, and Healthy Living. Unbridled one moment, perfectly functional the next, Mitz was a changeling. She handed Ona her new schedule with the words "Remedy for Academic Probation" scrawled at the top.

"You've got to face facts, Wisconsin. You're no genius."

By then, the real genius's cheekbones protruded, her hips jutted from the tops of her baggy jeans. Everything Mitz wouldn't eat went into Ona's mouth or Ona's still lifes: sushi, Thai noodles with peanut sauce, Italian plums that sat on Mitz's desk until Ona had eaten every last one. The less Mitz ate, the hungrier Ona grew. She packed on ten pounds, then five more. She loaded her shelves with boxes of macaroni and cookies and jars of olives, and she drew. Mitz would stand back and pretend to be a critic. She would stroke her chin. She would raise an eyebrow. "So visceral. So sublime. The lines. The chiaroscuro. The sauce!"

Onto the male figure. The model before Ona had a scar down his chest. He should have aged out of the system. No twenty-year-old wanted to draw his soft belly, his thinning hair. But everyone drew the scar. Ona heard the long, hatched line. The model heard it too. He pressed his lips into a proud curl. She wouldn't draw him like that, holding a metal rod like a spear. She drew him in a hospital bed instead, a nurse handing him his heart swaddled like a baby. Mitz again, despite the white uniform. And look, there was Ona's father sitting in the corner with his newspaper, and there was Mitz's mother in her long dress, waves rushing under the door, and there was the wholesome model from blind drawing. No, that was Ona, balancing on feet as enormous as boats.

"Time to move out of the food phase, Peaches," Mitz had said. "Try a blue period. Everyone does." Ona's early still lifes made Mitz so dizzy she tore them down. She sat on Ona's bed and put her head between her knees.

Ona told her it was time to see a doctor, but they decided to go to a bar instead. They squeezed together in their favorite booth. Ona ordered a Manhattan.

"How gauche," Mitz said. She ordered a Pabst. She spotted their friends Bobcat and Charlie across the room and called them over. She ate the cherry out of Ona's drink, ordered a pizza, invited the boys to their dorm room, and Ona thought it might be over. She might not have to call Mitz's parents, she might not have to listen to Mitz's pen scratching through the night.

In their room, Mitz said, "Let's smoke it under a blanket. Get the blanket, BobbieCat."

Mitz said, "Little Miss Peaches and Cream is high."

Mitz said, "Let's push the beds together. Let's go nighty-night."

Ona fell. Their beds were a raft. Now Mitz was making out

with Bobcat. Ona was twisted around Charlie. Bobcat said, "Holy shit, Mitz. You're like a skeleton. What the fuck." Mitz toppled into Ona. She was laughing. She was laughing so hard she was crying. "Get out," she said. "Now. Get out! Get out! Get out!" Mitz threw out Bobcat. She threw out Charlie. She threw out Ona. Ona lay down in the hall next to the door and held onto the doorknob. "Mitz," she yelled. "Let me in!"

Hundreds upon hundreds of Post-it notes in perfect lines all over their walls. Mitz said she just needed to get them into the right sequence. She just needed a little more caffeine. She told Ona her scalp tingled. Her heart pounded. She had stopped showering. At night, she rocked on her bed, working through her theory, starting over and over again. She rearranged the notes. Where was it? Where was the one about the gold standard and pattern language? She slept with the pages of her notebooks sticking to her face.

"I'm calling the RA," Ona said.

"Just a few more days," Mitz said. "I'm going to be all right. I know the drill. We just need the right recipe. See, you start with rice. Just white rice first, and then you build on that. I've got new pills. You're the only one who understands. Please, Ona. Just let me get through finals."

Ona found reasons to stay out of the room. She started seeing Nate Elkins, a golden-haired geology major with a penchant for Dylan. He drove her out to the country for hikes and lectured about rivers and accumulation, about erosion and sedimentary rock. "Whatever you do, don't talk to Mitz about erosion," Ona warned. "She's got enough on her mind."

For her political science exam, Mitz wrote in tiny handwriting and needed two additional blue books.

"They never give you enough time. No one values intellectual curiosity anymore," she said, when the test was returned with a failing mark and the words "convoluted" and "does not answer question." She took out another blue book and kneeled on the floor to finish.

Ona's father valued curiosity. When she told him she wanted to fly to the Southwest for winter break, he said, "You go right ahead. Live your life. There's nothing to see around here. Ticket's on me." She didn't tell him she was going with Nate Elkins, that it didn't matter who she was with or where, only that she was away. He said, "Is everything all right? You know, if there's anything you need."

Her mother said, "This might be his last Christmas. How could you, Ona?"

She'd never been west of the Mississippi. She'd never been on a plane. When she looked at the mountains below, she was free. When Nate squeezed her hand, she was free of Mitz. She wouldn't think of her, or of her father opening his presents, hanging the still life of plums Ona made for him above his new retractable bed.

Nate Elkins was so healthy he glowed. He called Ona his Girl from the North Country. She was pure, so lovely he could just about marry her. He brought Ona to his family's enormous winter "cottage" with its skylights and tiled veranda, and Ona thought, This must be what Mitz meant by new money.

"He's got that virgin/whore hang-up," Mitz said, when Ona returned. "Classic pastoral fantasy. Corn-fed-girl syndrome. It's in his DNA. He'll never get over it. Your mother keeps calling. It doesn't sound good."

"Things are going to be tight," her mother told her. "We're running out of options. We maxed out your dad's insurance. You'll have to find a job."

If only Ona hadn't borrowed so much money from Mitz. She promised herself she would take Mitz to the counseling center. She would get a new roommate. She would pay Mitz back.

But first she loaded their shelves with groceries. She didn't feel well, no matter how much she ate. When she opened their medicine cabinet, she found half-full bottles of medications prescribed to Mitz and Mitz's mother and someone named Susan Kim. She found empty laxative boxes in the garbage. Bottles of herbal remedies for heavy metal contamination and teas for mental confusion. She found a nest of Mitz's hair on the floor. "Look at this," she said to Mitz. "Whatever you're doing, it's not working. It's gone too far. I'm calling your mom."

But then Ona missed her period again, and Mitz was so calm, so Mitz, so suddenly levelheaded. "But of course," she said, as she pulled the birth control packet out of Ona's purse and pointed to the uneven pattern of holes. "What did you expect? Did you think you were immune?"

*

At the clinic, Mitz held Ona's hand while the nurse took a sonogram. "I think you're having a fish," she said. "A rockfish. Definitely a rockheadfish."

The nurse stared at Mitz.

"Rockhead, get it?" Mitz said. "Her boyfriend is into geology?"

The nurse turned to Ona and pointed to a picture of a ten-week-old fetus on a chart. She lectured Ona on the importance of not drinking and staying out of hot tubs. "We'll need to see you in another four weeks," she said. "I can also give you a referral to a counselor, if you'd like."

"I told you we're both clichés," Mitz said on the way home. "You can't keep it, you know. Or you could, but either way it's no good. You'll be the tragic townie who fell for the rich boy. He'll freak. He only pretends to be progressive."

Then the bleeding began, in their room, the next night.

"I'm taking you to the hospital. You're running a fever. We should call your mother."

"I'm so stupid. Please, Mitz, I'll be all right. I promise, I won't call your parents, if you don't call mine."

Mitz helped Ona into bed. She gave her antibiotics from her arsenal in the medicine cabinet. She took Ona's temperature and helped her to the bathroom. She held her when she cried. She told Nate that Ona had the flu and he should keep away, and he must have known, because he did, for days and days.

When Ona woke from the fever, she was fired clean. There was no more turbulence in her mind, no more hunger. Then Nate came by with a milk shake. He kissed her forehead. He told her she would always be his Girl from the North Country, but they had to talk. Things had changed.

So this is what it meant to haunt a room. Ona and Mitz skipped classes. They fought about the mess. Then they stopped talking to each other. They pulled their beds to separate corners and put on headphones and ignored each other until the quiet erupted into slammed doors and windows opening and closing.

Then Ona left. She hung out in cafés and bars. She didn't come home for days. She brought men back to their room and asked Mitz to sleep in the lounge.

"This is ridiculous," Mitz said. "It's textbook, you know."

"You're just pissed because they don't come running to you anymore. Here, Mitz, have a cookie." Ona threw a carton from the nightstand.

She expected Mitz to lob the cookies back. She had witnessed Mitz's most spectacular and regal tantrums, had watched her turn purple and listened as her voice reached terrifying octaves over nothing more than her parents' refusal to buy her a new laptop. But Mitz didn't throw anything now. She just crumpled onto the bed and cried into her pillow.

Then Ona's father died.

"A good man. He'd give you the shirt off his back," they told Ona and her mother and brother, one after another, in the church basement after the funeral.

The good man was buried in a silver casket the undertaker

convinced Ona's mother to buy. Her father would have had a joke for this too, and she almost heard him whisper it into her ear. During the wake, he looked like he was sleeping in a metal canoe, and Ona thought how wrong it was that a man who spent his last years fighting for breath should be buried underground.

"We took out a second mortgage," her mother said. "There's nothing left. He didn't want you to know, but you're an adult now. I think you know what this means."

Everything was so intermingled. Mitz helped Ona sort her books and clothes from her own. They carried Ona's belongings to the parking lot and loaded her father's Buick. Mitz struggled with the boxes. She had been sick for weeks, first a cold and then pneumonia. She was seeing a therapist, but not telling her much. Standing in the parking lot, in her ragged sweater and long skirt, the snow coming down like dust, she reminded Ona of a consumption patient from the nineteenth century.

"You know I'm going to let you go," Mitz said. "I'm not going to make a scene. I'm going to stand here and watch with no expression at all, and when you disappear down the road, I'll still be here."

"Please don't hug me," she said, when Ona reached out her arms.

"I'm sorry," Ona said. "About everything. You'll come and see me?"

Mitz raised her hand in a mock wave. "I'm going to pretend

to smile. I'm going to pretend to wave. It will be very Lars von Trier."

When Ona called several months after her move, it was Mitz's new roommate who told her Mitz was gone. "She almost died, you know."

Mitz wouldn't leave the room, that's what the roommate said. She smelled bad. She wouldn't turn off her lights at night. She covered the walls with *Post-its*!

"A stroke. Can you believe it? She weighed ninety pounds. I don't know if she was anorexic or just crazy. All I know is I don't blame you for leaving. I don't care what people say."

Sometimes Mitz still talked to her when Ona was alone and painting.

For instance, she might say, "Maybe all those times you think you see your father, it really is your father. Like, maybe he's just checking up on you."

"But what about you? I see you too. Just yesterday, that girl standing in line at the movies."

"Oh, that was just your guilt. It's ridiculous, by the by. We make our own fortunes, our own beds. Sow what you reap and all. Isn't that funny? All those words for the same thing, but it mostly comes down to luck. And genetics."

Ona would call her senior exhibition "Mitz's Endless Theory of Everything." She would cover the wall with miniature paintings, from ceiling to floor, just like Mitz's Post-it notes.

"It will be an inside joke though," Mitz said. "And no one likes those."

Ona called Simone again. "Will you call me as soon as you find her? I'm worried too, you know."

"You're worried too? You *colluded* with her. You *lied* to us when we could have helped her. I'm going to hang up. I can't do this now."

"Please. I just want to talk to her. You'll tell her, when she comes back?"

"I'm going to say something I shouldn't, Ona. I don't like you. I don't trust you. I know it's unfair. I know I'm not blameless, but I'll always associate you with this. You were supposed to be her friend."

From across the gallery, Ona spied Mitz wearing lipstick and a sleek trench coat, like this was a fancy Manhattan opening. Ona's heart pounded. Her mouth was dry. She was afraid Mitz would disappear if she looked away. She watched Mitz pass several student exhibits and stop before a gigantic painting of a purple vulva that reminded Ona of the entrance to a tourist trap in the Dells. Mitz raised an eyebrow at Ona and mouthed *Oh my god.*

Then she circled a tower fashioned entirely of illuminated X-rays, fishing wire, and bleached bones. Mitz turned to watch the crowd. She gazed at disoriented parents, mothers with too-wide smiles, fathers in uncomfortable suits. She watched a rural couple pose for a photo with their son as she made her way to Ona.

Ona knew she wouldn't really be there, but she reached out for her anyway.

"You're seeing things again," Mitz said. She gazed at Ona's paintings.

Ona had managed to cram seventeen canvases into her limited space. "There's no focal point," Mitz said. "And don't tell me that was your intention." She read Ona's artist statement. "At least you didn't use the words *liminal* or *intertextual*."

Several people glanced from Ona's work to Ona.

"Say something. You're scaring them," Mitz whispered. "By the by, I think I'm touched, but I'm not sure. You did a fine job of capturing the pathos, but next time I want boobs."

"Disturbing," a woman said, as she looked at Ona's sketch of two skeletal women tangled together on a doll-sized bed, men flat as rugs on either side.

"You had to be there," Mitz told the woman. "It was a lot more fun than it looks."

Mitz stepped closer to the painting of a fat girl holding a bean-sized baby in her oversized palm. "It won't work, you know," she said to Ona. "You can't fall apart. Even if you try."

Then she was gone. She didn't slip into the crowd or vanish through a wall. She was simply not there.

If Ona could just find Mitz, she'd tell her she finally understood the problems of relative distance and sampling from the whole. Mere arrangement would never suffice.

A few days before they parted, Mitz removed her notes from their walls. She told Ona she was "on the mend," though it was clear this was just another respite, and Ona knew if she opened Mitz's desk drawer the notes would be there, stacked and waiting.

That night, before bed, Mitz opened the window. "Smell that air," she said. "Now we'll sleep." She didn't wrestle with her sheets or get up repeatedly to use the bathroom or wake Ona to tell her about a possible link between gray matter and the metric expansion of space.

"I can hear you thinking," Mitz said. "Tell me about that night again. Tell me about the ice."

Once, when Ona was eight and she and her father couldn't sleep, he took her out to the river to skate. Mitz loved the story. She liked the idea of Ona's father shoveling to make a rink. She liked the detail of his sinking a Coleman lantern into a snowbank. But most of all, she liked to imagine the sound of ice cracking, like far-off gunshots coming close.

"My dad said it was the river breathing. But that made it worse. I kept thinking of a monster down there, trying to get out."

"The ice monster of Wisconsin. I love it. Do you think it wears a hat with earflaps?" They laughed and said goodnight. Several minutes later, Mitz said, "Probably forms in layers, like glaciers, or tectonic plates."

Toward morning, Ona woke convinced Mitz was at her desk writing. But when she sat up, it was just Mitz's heavy coat hanging from her chair. Mitz was sleeping. Her back was to Ona, her knees pulled to her chest. She mumbled something. Ona could smell rotting leaves from the open window, new cardboard from her packed boxes. In that half-light, the cold blowing in, she could almost hear crabs scuttling across the ocean floor, rice growing in distant fields, the universe expanding around them.

Then Mitz turned toward Ona. Her eyes were open and staring, though she was still asleep. Her arm slipped over the edge of her bed and hung there. "Turn off the music," she said. "We're almost there."

THE ONLY THING MISSING WAS THE HOWLING OF WOLVES

HOW COULD MY SISTER, CRAZY AS THEY COME, STILL COERCE ME into doing things that could come to no good? She had her two-year-old grandson, Wendell, in her arms, and he was wearing a baptismal gown, and she was saying, "Just this once, Harlan. I got it all worked out. No one will ever know, except me and you and the good Lord. You won't have to do a darn thing except drive."

Lynette had lost her driver's license years ago, and one of her Narconon friends had dropped her and the kid off at my house in the country. There I was trying to install her borrowed car seat in my pickup, so I could take her back home. She was like the wild mint in the garden I couldn't eradicate. It kept coming up, sucking the nourishment from everything I planted. Then she was handing me Wendell, installing that seat as if she were born to such things.

We got into the truck and she said, "Can't you just feel it? Them birds out there and that breeze? That's God, Harlan. That's God on our side."

I pulled away as she stuck her head out the open window and let her newly dyed hair blow. In the backseat, Wendell laughed, and I had to look away from the rearview. In that lacy gown with his fine hair slicked to one side, his eyes set too close together, I had to agree with Lynette that his name was a tragedy in the making. She refused to call him Wendell, preferring Scotty Boy instead.

"How do you like me as a brunette, Harlan? You didn't even say nothing."

For once her face wasn't made up with three layers of paint. She wore a blue dress buttoned primly over her tattoos, not the usual tight shirt and shorts, and I remembered her at seventeen, pregnant and leaving home with nothing but a pillowcase stuffed with clothes. I was fourteen then, and now here we were again, both of us, forty-six years later back in our hometown in Wisconsin.

We passed a highway patrolman clocking traffic from his car and she ducked out of sight.

God had set the whole thing in motion, she had said. Ross's wife had called her in a moment of desperation, needing a sitter. We'd have just enough time to get the kid up to a chapel in the woods for a christening she had just that morning arranged, if only I would take her.

"How'd you get the kid, Lynette?" The last time we talked, she told me Ross had stopped speaking to her.

She sat up and pretended to notice the Watsons' hobby farm. Just last week, they'd purchased two emus. "Holy crap," she said. "What is that? Is that an ostrich?"

I stopped in the middle of the road, and she braced her hands on the dashboard and looked behind us.

"I asked you how you got him?"

"From his daycare, what'd you think? That I kidnapped

him?" She made her voice high and whiny and mimicked Wendell's daycare teacher. "You aren't on our list of approved caretakers. As a matter of fact, you are on our list of people who are not allowed to see Wendell. Me. *His own grandmother.* Can you believe it? I *sacrificed*, Harlan. I gave Ross up so he could live in that big house and never even think of me."

We were just two miles from town. I started driving again, slowly, and strained my ears. I thought I heard sirens, and I pulled onto a tractor path that led into a cornfield so I could think. Wendell was strangely quiet, and Lynette noticed me watching him in the rearview.

"I just gave him a little Benadryl," she said. "Just to relax him. He won't be any trouble and we'll have him back in a jiffy."

"Don't say another word, Lynette. I don't want to know anything else."

By now the daycare had called Ross, and Ross had called the cops. Soon someone would put two and two together, and they'd be looking for me too.

"Someday they're gonna write about me, Harlan. You could be part of history too, part of the underground baptism railroad. They're everywhere, people just like me. Only I'll be like the Mother of the Railroad."

"You kidnapped him, Lynette. That's a felony."

"Stupid daycare people. I would of never put Ross or Caleb there. I left them with people I knew."

Ross had told me about some of the people Lynette left them with—biker chicks high on speed, a senile neighbor, men she'd known for a few days. She had lived on a commune near

Nashville. She had helped run a bar out in Wyoming. She had hitchhiked with her kids across the country, losing her youngest in an apartment fire in Eugene, Oregon, while she was out partying, then giving her son Ross to an aunt to raise back home.

"Do you have any idea how much trouble you're making? I don't need this now, Lynette."

Lynette turned in her seat and gave me a hard stare. "I ain't doing this for you, Harlan. I'm doing this for Scotty Boy." Her voice lowered and she shuddered as she talked about how the world was dying of spiritual decay because of our generation, and how it was time for us to stick out our necks and take a stand.

Let me tell you about our generation, I wanted to say. While you were swallowing tabs of acid and partying, I was on a gunboat dodging sniper fire from the banks of Song Cau Lon.

She went on and on about birds that fell from the sky and dead fish that washed to shore, how we'd polluted and destroyed everything, all for the love of money. "Kids like Scotty are in for a world of hurt," she said. "Because of us, Harlan."

All that was left of her lipstick was an orange outline. Her mouth wouldn't stop moving, the wind blew the tall and browning corn. A flock of crows rose from the field. The weather, the scenery, everything was just a bit too sharp. I knew it from my time in the service and from years of trucking—days like these were specially crafted for the worst kind of trouble.

"I didn't kidnap him, Harlan. Scotty was outside with his little friends and he came right to me, just slipped right through the fence. I didn't do a thing except ask if he wanted to meet our good Lord and be beloved and safe. And he said, 'OK, Gamma. OK.' So I took him and we ran."

"He's two years old."

"Pardon me, Harlan, but *I* happen to know a thing or two about two-year-olds."

I had a son once too, but his heart shut down and he only lived for a day. I was remarried, living in Baltimore and starting college. My new wife and I came home from the hospital and one of the neighbors had hung a big, blue Welcome, Baby sign above our front door. For a long time no one except my wife's parents came to see us. My mother just sent a card, saying it was God's will. Lynette, if she ever knew, never called or wrote. She had problems of her own by then. I quit school and started trucking, and before long my wife met someone else. I wish I could say that this had been the beginning of the bad streak, but as far back as I could remember it had been there, persistent and unpredictable, just like Lynette.

I backed down the path and was almost to the road when two squad cars roared by. Lynette clutched the fabric of her dress and looked out the back window. "They'll ruin everything," she said. She reminded me of our mother then, her hands clenched, always looking up at the sky as if it were full of locusts.

"You just can't leave anyone alone," I said. "You messed up Ross's life. Now you want to fuck up Wendell's and mine too."

"Harlan, you better watch your language." She looked upward like God was listening. "You can't see right no more. It ain't your fault. You got everything you need now. You got that house Carla just give to you, clean out of the blue, though you never did nothing for her. You got that plot out back to grow things in and a truck and a tractor too. You got everything, and I ain't never said a bad thing about it to you. The least you can do is help me with this one last thing. Then I'll leave you alone. I won't tell nobody anymore I'm your sister. I won't ever ask you for nothing, not ever again."

I should have known she'd use my moving into my first wife's house against me. I had married Carla right out of high school and divorced her as soon as I was out of the service. She never remarried, grew old like the rest of us, lost all her family over the years, and lived in the same ranch house her father bought for us on the other side of town. I stopped once to see her on a route west, and we talked over coffee. She still kept our wedding picture in her china hutch. As I was leaving she hugged me and told me she was glad I was getting to see the country. "You did good, Harlan. Maybe you'll send me pictures of your babies when you have them," she said, and I broke down and cried and told her about my son, about his tiny fingernails, about his ears shaped just like mine, and she led me to the bedroom and I slept through the night and I lost my job because of it. Then years later she willed me the house, *out of the blue*, as Lynette would say.

By now every officer in town was looking for us. There was probably an Amber Alert. I couldn't bear to look at Wendell. We'd had him for less than an hour and he was groggy and his hair was slick with sweat. He mumbled the beginning of the alphabet song, ADBC, over and over, reversing the letters, making strange motions with his hands. Something was wrong with him, and I knew, despite what Lynette said, that his parents were right in taking him to therapy twice a week.

"Well," Lynette said. "Are you going to help us or not?"

She reminded me how she carted me everywhere in a wagon when I was young. "I wasn't no bigger than you," she said. "Mom had left again. You don't remember that, but I do. You took a can of tar from the shed and poured it all over the kitchen. I had to cut it out of your hair. I told Dad I did it."

I considered driving straight into the corn or dropping her and the kid at a farmhouse, leaving town, never coming back. I could still see her just as she was back then, the police car parked in front of our house, her lying to our father, telling him she had been the one to make me steal the candy, the comic books, the records, and all the other things I couldn't keep my hands from taking and stuffing into my mouth or under my shirt. I stole, and she slept with every boy in town. All through childhood she had stood before our father, telling me with her eyes to let her do the talking.

I hesitated too long. She put her hand on my arm. "Can't you just do this one little thing? We'll take the side roads. They'll never find us. It's not like we're going to murder him or something."

I told myself it didn't matter if we turned back now or later, as long as she didn't implicate me. "I had nothing to do with this," I said. "I know nothing about a baptism, nothing about the daycare. As far as I know, we're just going for a drive."

I pulled onto the highway and headed out of town, and

Lynette threw her arms around me and kissed my cheek. "It ain't far," she said. "I got the directions right here," and she pointed to her head.

We'd been driving north on a county road alongside 51, through wasting towns, past lonesome dogs and pitiful yard sales, when Lynette finally admitted we were lost. I could no longer pretend I wanted to turn around because when I stopped at an all-in-one gas station, its shelves filled with automotive parts in aging packaging next to yellowed cartons of cereal, I felt the familiar thrill of getting away with something. I bought baseball caps and sunglasses to disguise Lynette and Wendell, diapers and chocolate milk and animal crackers for the kid, snacks for Lynette and me, and I had a shoddy grin on my face, just like when I was a kid, sauntering out of the five-and-dime with two Clark bars and a pack of baseball cards shoved into my coat.

The man behind the counter had a face gray as granite. In his greasy front pocket were a pack of Pall Malls and an open box of Milk Duds. I asked for directions to the chapel in Williams, and he stretched out a sun-blackened arm and pointed to a spot near the state forest on a map taped to the counter. "Pretty near a ghost town now," he said as he chewed and cleaned his teeth with his tongue. "Water ain't right on account of them mines. Company keeps saying they're gonna clean it up. Believe it when I see it."

I paid and he tossed everything into a sack. "Lost two kids up there last year," he said. "Didn't find them until after the thaw.

Fell into one of them shafts from up above. Snow covered the hole right up. Entire town went out looking with sticks, poking through the woods and all. Thought some crazy took them." The man lifted his cap to scratch his head and then set it back down. He told me about the bad winter, how the snow drifted over the gas pump handles and shut down the highway. "You know what they say," he said. "The only thing missing was the howling of wolves."

I stared again at the map. "What about back roads?"

The man pulled out a magnifying glass and passed it over the map. He pointed to a winding road west of the main highway. "Slow you down some," he said. "Ain't nothing that way except jackrabbits and drunks till you get to Chatawaska."

"Will you look at all these goodies," Lynette said, when I returned to the truck. "Harlan got you some yummy crackers, kiddo." She put the hat on him and turned the bill to the side, and Wendell grabbed it and threw it off. "Don't exactly match his dress, Harlan," she said.

"When were you going to tell me that Williams is all the way up in Michigan?"

"Michigan!" She widened her eyes to mock me, and then she ripped open the animal crackers. She held one out to me teasingly, then bit off its head. "Don't you feel cleaner already, Harlan? Working in the service of the Lord?"

"More like the devil," I said, and she laughed.

We headed northeast on a county road where pastures

turned to forest and the few houses we saw were hunting shacks or an occasional trailer peeking from the woods. The whole state was going to hell. Our own town had lost a third of its population in less than a decade. Most, like my nephew Ross, lived in new developments outside of town and commuted to the nearest city.

We came across a state park with a broken chain across the entrance and a "closed for the winter" sign, though it was summer. I drove over the chain and down a dirt road to an overgrown clearing with a picnic table and two outhouses. At the table, Lynette marched animal crackers toward the boy and jumped them into his mouth, and he laughed hysterically. He had come out of his daze and was happier outside in the breeze.

Lynette wandered into the field to pick wildflowers, Wendell toddling behind her in his gown stained with chocolate milk. I could hear the rushing of a stream beyond the field. I sat under a willow, watching a hawk circle overhead and before I knew it, I was dreaming I had to run a shipment through Stevens Pass, the road slick with mud, my wheels sliding as I careened down the mountain.

And then Lynette was standing over me, mascara smeared under her eyes, grass sticking to her cheek. "Wake up, Harlan. I can't find him. I can't find him anywhere."

The sun was lower in the sky and the air, cooler. I took off toward the road and Lynette followed, yelling, "Scotty Boy," and then "Wendell. Wendell!" I could hear my heart in my throat as I ran.

Lynette was right behind me. She tugged at my shirt. "We

were just going to lie down for a little. I thought it would help me remember the directions."

"Go look for him," I said. I imagined us in a courtroom, Ross pointing at me from behind the witness stand, his wife tearing at her hair. I ran one direction and then the other. I went into the outhouses and looked inside the toilets, down into the muck.

I tore across the field and Lynette followed. "Get out of my sight," I said. "This is all on you."

The grass was too tall for a toddler. I felt the ground with my boots, prayed I would find him in the weeds, a clump of black-eyed Susans in his fist. The world was a horrible, dangerous place. There was no way to keep it away. I pushed through brush to the bank of the creek. The current was high and fast. I had to tear my eyes from a long branch caught between two rocks. "Wendell!" I shouted.

Lynette stood knee-deep in the creek, staring at the water rushing around her calves. I heard a screech from downstream. Lynette looked up, and I ran toward the sound, and there was Wendell sitting in the mud, off from a bare spot on the bank. He stood and fell back down, his gown wet and clinging to him. His face was red and angry. I scooped him into my arms. His diaper hung from him, and his legs were covered with scratches and a half dozen leeches. Water poured down my shirt. "Up, me up," he said, which I took to mean "put me down," but I held him tighter and took him back to the truck, Lynette walking alongside, reaching out her arms.

"Get a diaper," I barked, slamming down the back gate of the truck.

Now that we found him, the years boiled out. I made Wendell lie down on the truck bed. He fought me with his legs and arms. I held him down as Lynette pulled off his diaper and put on a new disposable one from the shopping bag. She had never even thought of packing a change of clothing. She was making faces at Wendell, saying, "Look at that little, wittle nose, those little, wittle ears."

I took Wendell's gown and wrenched it over his head and threw it at Lynette, saying, "Wring it out." Then I told her to hold him, and I got matches from the glove compartment.

"What do you want with those?" she said, and she looked frightened.

"We're going to burn it all," I said. "Get rid of everything, live off the land."

Her eyes widened.

"Leeches," I said. "Or didn't you notice?"

Wendell cried silently now. Lynette patted his new diaper and made him sit up and pulled the gown back over his head, the fabric so cold and unforgiving, he shuddered. "You're a Wigby, just like us," she said, although Ross had changed his last name. "Now hold still. Be tough."

I lit one match at a time and blew it out before touching it to a fat leech and the kid just watched. He didn't say a word. Lynette pulled them off one at a time and dropped them to the ground. She wiped her hands on her dress and carried Wendell back to his car seat.

I took some burlap I had in back for my plants and covered him, and then Lynette and I got into the truck. The burlap was too rough and Wendell pulled it off. I buried my head in my arms over the steering wheel and closed my eyes.

"I'm sorry, Harlan," Lynette said. "I never do nothing right. I give up. Let's go home."

"You want to go home? Sure. Why not?" I turned the truck around and sped out of the park. Wendell laughed at every bump, and I made my voice ugly and high and pleading. "It's all our fault, Harlan. We've got to save him, Harlan. Jesus has got to save him. It's up to us, Harlan."

Lynette held onto the door handle with both hands. "Stop that, Harlan. You stop."

And then I did stop. I slammed on my brakes, and the kid started crying all over again.

"What happened to you, Harlan? I don't even know you no more."

I couldn't tell her about the years living in motels, stealing from the back of trucks, the money I stole from my last boss, the lost years, the fact that I sold plants at the market and took odd jobs because no one would ever employ me again.

"You can tell me anything, Harlan," Lynette said, turning around to wipe Wendell's nose. "I'm your sister. I would understand."

"They'll never let you see him again," I said. "You know that, don't you?"

"I know it," she said. "They don't let me see him anyway. If I could have, I would have done it without you. I would have done it on my own."

We drove another forty miles northwest through a tunnel of skinny pines, neither of us saying a word, Wendell asleep, and then a sign appeared for a fish hatchery and Lynette shouted, "That's it! We're almost there. Take a right onto that road." She opened the window to get a better look, and Wendell woke and squinted at the fiery peach of the setting sun.

At a sign painted with the words Back Woods Ministry, I turned onto a narrow dirt road. "It better be open," I said.

Lynette pulled down the visor mirror to fix her hair. "It ain't a Walmart, Harlan. It's a church. They have to stay open."

Every fifty feet or so another sign appeared, the letters misshapen and trailing upward, as if painted by a child: *And He drove him into the wilderness. Mark 1:12. Here is the king you have chosen. Samuel 12:13.*

Lynette pulled her Bible out of her purse and held it against her chest. In the woods, with the smell of balsam around us, the sun glinting behind the trees, it was almost like we were settlers in the New World, and for the first time in a long time, I wanted something to believe in too.

The road widened and stopped. Before us was Lynette's cathedral in the woods, though it was just a pine cabin on a concrete foundation, its windows dark, a log cross rising before it. The carved door was its only ornamentation. There was just enough daylight to make out Jesus sinking under the weight of a cross, an angel with feathered wings soaring above.

"You better wait here," Lynette said. She walked across the dirt lot, bowing her head and batting her arms at a cloud of wasps that guarded the door. She pulled on the handle, but it wouldn't open, and then she rushed back.

"One of them stung me," she said, getting back in beside me, and she sucked at a welt on her arm. "Maybe somebody's in that house."

I hadn't noticed the shack behind the church. The entire place had the feeling of abandonment. Lynette reached behind her for the burlap and wrapped it around herself before getting out again and opening the side door for Wendell. "Oh, Scotty," she said. "Look at your dress." She wrapped the two of them in the burlap for protection and made her way behind the church.

I dodged the wasps and followed. A blue tarp was nailed over a large hole in the roof of the house. Someone had taped cardboard over one of the front windows. Lynette knocked on the door. Robed in that burlap with Wendell pressed to her, she almost looked like the Virgin herself.

After several long moments, the door opened and out stepped a gangly preacher, exactly the kind you'd expect in such a place. He had a huge cranium and wild hair, and he looked as if he hadn't slept in years. He said nothing, just stepped aside.

Lynette went in first. She stood just inside the room,

removing the cloth and setting Wendell down. He sat at her feet on the wood floor and pulled off his remaining shoe.

"We're here for the baptism," she said. Her voice was soft, her expression flat, as it always was when she was afraid. "We got lost."

The room had almost no furniture, just two plastic lawn chairs and a giant beanbag. I wanted to see the preacher sit on that beanbag, and I pictured him there in the evening, his long legs and giant feet sprawled in front of him as he worked on a sermon. On one wall was the outline of a now missing cross. In the far corner was an old television with rabbit ear antennas. There were piles of yellow legal pads filled with scrawling and next to them an open can of corn with a fork in it.

The preacher sat down on one of the chairs. Lynette's eyes darted back and forth, taking in the room, and then she sat on the beanbag and tried to hold herself erect. I sat down on the other chair, and Wendell came to me and pulled on my pant leg. "We go," he said. "Out. Go outside." I put him on my lap and held him, and I wanted to have never brought him here. His cheek was scratched. His eyes were red-rimmed and his scalp smelled of algae and sour milk. He wrenched away and picked up his shoe and returned again. "Outside," he said. "Go outside."

The pastor looked at Lynette, then at me. We were too old to have such a young child. "It's late," he said. "Why don't you come back next weekend?"

"Next weekend?" I said. "You mean to tell me you got something better to do? What kind of scam is this you're running, anyway?"

"Don't, Harlan," Lynette said, and to the preacher, "He's tired from driving."

The preacher scratched his long, bony nose and seemed to be seeing Wendell for the first time. He took in the boy's soiled gown, his tear-streaked face, his naked feet.

"Would you excuse me a moment," he said. He walked out of the house towards the church.

"There's no underground railroad, is there Lynette?"

"You better get out of here, Harlan. Take your truck. Me and Wendell, we won't rat you out. I give up. Somebody ought to just shoot me."

Without saying good-bye, I walked outside. It was getting dark. The wasps were asleep. I could have driven away, but a light came through the open back door of the church. The preacher stood in a small office, staring into the night, the phone under his hand on a cluttered desk.

I stepped inside and he backed away, and I saw what he saw, a potentially violent child abductor. "Put that phone down. Now," I said.

He dropped his hands to his sides and stood looking at me, unblinking, unsurprised. I said, "Sit down," and when he did, I told him how all her life Lynette took the ugly and pretended it was beautiful, and how seeing the beautiful had led her astray again and again. I told him she had once wrecked her car in Arizona and when she crawled out and walked along the road she thought she saw an angel in a long coat, telling her to stop drugging and to *go forth*. I told him some of us refused the beautiful, and that was a problem too. I said I knew something about this, and I thought he did too. I told him how Lynette had left her nine-year-old son in an apartment with her older one while she went out drinking, and how she had come back to find the entire building in flames and couldn't find him, not among the survivors. I told him how she lay awake at night thinking about that son, out in limbo, wandering and motherless, her other son forever broken, how she needed to baptize Wendell not to make everything all right, but just a bit better. Lynette often said that depression was what happened when you couldn't work yourself to death, when there wasn't a substance left on the planet that could take you away from your own mind, when you hadn't found Jesus, or Jesus hadn't found you. I said, sometimes a man hides from trouble, and sometimes a man goes looking for it because he can't resist its pull, because trouble is a release of sorts. I told him he had opened the door to trouble just now, as I had that morning, and I knew he wanted to let it in, I knew he needed to finish letting it in.

The pastor listened. All around him were half-packed boxes of papers and framed family pictures. I wondered how he'd lost his congregation and how long it took. I mused at how like Lynette it was to find a place like this. Then I remembered the story the gas station man told me, about boys falling into a mine right there in Williams, and I read the preacher's dull gaze and knew if I looked in those boxes I'd find pictures of those boys. "At least give us a head start," I said. "Let me take them back."

"I won't put anything on paper," he said. "And I don't do baptisms in the church anymore."

*

By the light of a Coleman lantern, he led us to the river behind the church. Lynette carried Wendell. He was half asleep and heavy in her arms. We followed the preacher to the bank where he waded to his knees through the current, just beyond several large rocks where the water lost its wildness but grew deeper. I raised the lantern for him and thought of the painting my mother had hanging in our kitchen, of Puritans crossing an angry river. The lantern swayed and momentarily lit our figures, turning the woods to shadow.

The pastor's voice was too loud for the night. "I tell you the truth," he said. "No one can enter the kingdom of God unless he is born of water…." He recited a few more lines and then waved Lynette forward. Wendell's head was against her shoulder, but when the cold water met his bare feet, he began to cry and thrash, and she nearly lost hold of him. Her wet skirt wrapped around her legs and she stood swaying in the water, unable or unwilling to bring the child. The preacher waited, impatient or unbelieving or just weary. He trudged through the water and took Wendell from Lynette. "No one can enter," I heard again and again, though he said it just once.

Wendell gripped the preacher's shirt. The preacher tipped him backwards and poured water over his forehead, and Wendell closed his eyes and convulsed. He stretched out his legs and arms. He was silent for a second, then he was reaching for Lynette, and Lynette was rushing forward, slipping, picking herself back up. "Gamma's here," she cried, but the pastor didn't trust her. He pressed Wendell against his chest and carried him to the bank where he handed him to me and took his lantern.

Wendell clung to me, and then all resistance left his body. I turned and cradled him back to the truck. He was shivering and too light in my arms. In the back seat, while Lynette paid the preacher, I dried Wendell the best I could, fastened his seatbelt, and covered him again with the burlap. Then Lynette and I got into the truck, and I turned on my headlights and started the engine.

Holding that lantern, his face furrowed and gaunt, the preacher looked like an angel of death. Lynette closed her eyes and sank into her seat as I backed up and headed away from that leaning cross and that dark church, down the path to the road. Lynette's hair was dripping and her arms were covered in gooseflesh. She glanced behind her at Wendell and turned to cover him again. "I'm sorry, baby," she whispered. This time Wendell didn't push the cloth away. He stared ahead as if emptied, and then his head bobbed forward, and he slept.

Nearly all the way back, no one said a word. We had hours to think, hours to listen to Wendell whimper and fall back to sleep. Lynette stared at the dark window. I watched the shoulders of the road for darting animals and turned on the radio, and for a while home was far away.

In the development where Ross lived, the houses were nearly identical and similar shades of beige. I thought I could find his house without rousing Lynette, but then she opened her eyes and said, "You got to turn into that cul-de-sac." She didn't have to tell me more because parked outside one of the houses was an empty police car, and inside all the lights were on.

"You better drop us off here," she said.

I pulled over and she got out and opened the side door and lifted Wendell out of his seat. "I'm sorry, Harlan, about all this. Including when you were little. I should have looked after you. I should have called."

She made her way down the street toward Ross's tri-level. Two unluckies, she and Wendell both. I imagined her in front of her burning apartment building all those years ago, being held back by a fireman, her son Ross beside her, looking into the flames. I saw myself leading Suzanne to the grave of our new son, and Carla, the woman who gave me everything she owned, dying alone in a hospital bed before her time. I imagined the preacher leading his congregation for days on a search through the woods for those missing boys.

I called to Lynette and ran to catch up with her. I took Wendell from her, and we walked together.

"Go home, Harlan," she said, but we climbed the front steps, and I breathed in Wendell's hair one last time. Lynette knocked on the door, and when it opened, Ross's wife shouted and took hold of Wendell, and Wendell burrowed himself into her. Then he pulled back to look at his mother's face. He wrapped his fist in her hair and pressed his cheek to her neck, and she began to cry, and she rushed him down a hallway to his room. Then Ross was shouting. He pushed at Lynette, and a police officer tried to hold him back. "What the fuck, Mom," he yelled. "What the fuck, Lynette," and he was crying too.

Lynette shrank against the wall and held her head with her hands. "He's OK," she said. "We didn't hurt him. We made him safe for you, Ross."

Ross turned to me, and before I could open my mouth, Lynette said, "It weren't Harlan. It weren't his idea. All he did was drive."

The cop took a small notepad from his uniform pocket and told us to start from the beginning. And just like when we were kids, I looked at Lynette, and she looked back at me. We conspired without saying a word. *You promised*, I said. *I know it*, she said. *It ends right here, Lynette. Yes, Harlan. With you and me.*

A HABIT OF SEEING

THE ENERGY OF THE BABY SHOWER REMINDED JULIA OF *Twelve Angry Men*. They were sitting around the dining table in Betsy's townhouse in the suburbs of Ann Arbor, arguing about parenting. Besides Betsy, there were several colleagues from the private high school where Julia taught acting and musical theatre. Julia's sister Sloane was in from Connecticut. And Sharon. She was back from Europe for the summer and looked like she wanted to hang herself on the line of baby clothes strung across the room as decor.

Sloane was saying, "Come on. Does Julia seem like the attachment type to you?"

"But it's only natural," Claire said. She had taken several years off from teaching to raise her two children and now worked as a substitute teacher.

"Look," Sloane said. "If we were meant to have our kids around our necks twenty-four hours a day, we'd have pouches like kangaroos."

"But we do," Claire said. "We have two arms. We have breasts."

Rick, the only man at the party and a good friend of Julia's from school, cleared his throat.

"You know what I mean," Claire said.

Betsy laughed nervously. "Stop it you guys. You're scaring Julia."

Sharon glanced at Julia, a smirk rising to her lips. Just three summers ago, she and Julia, and later Betsy, had waited tables together. Now Betsy was newly married and managing a hotel downtown, Sharon was trying to move back to Berlin for good, and Julia's husband Robert had found a permanent position at a local community college. Julia was glad he had decided not to come.

Rick said, "Is there going to be any booze or is this one of those dry showers?"

Julia pushed herself up from the head of the table. At seven months, she felt waterlogged and huge, the baby's head pressing against her bladder. "Betsy, where's that punch?" She wished she could have a drink too.

"You sit down, Julia," Betsy said. She rushed into the kitchen and returned with the punch bowl. Then she pulled out a bottle of vodka and said, "Keep this away from Julia!"

"Yes," Sharon said. "Especially if you have a piano."

Everyone turned to stare at Sharon. She spoke in an affected, droll tone now, though she was from a small town just a few hours away.

"This sounds like a story we need to hear," Rick said.

Julia's sister shifted uncomfortably in her seat. Like Sharon, she knew too much of Julia's past: being carted off by her mother to one casting call after another, swallowing a bottle of sleeping pills at thirteen, living with a coke-dealer playwright in Queens and having an abortion at nineteen, calling off a lavish wedding at the last minute to run off with Robert.

"Betsy," Julia said. "Didn't you say there would be games?"

They gathered in the living room to spoon cotton balls out of a bowl while blindfolded. When it was her turn, Julia pretended to stumble around. She could see through the thin scarf, but she set to work on the cotton balls, surprised at how much she wanted to beat the highest score. The cotton was so light it slipped from the spoon. If she hadn't been able to see through the material, she wouldn't have gotten any at all.

One by one, they played, until Betsy tied the blindfold around Sharon, and Sharon made her way forward with the spoon and then stopped herself. She pulled off the cloth. "I can see through it."

"Could everyone see?" Betsy asked.

There was a collective groan.

"Prize goes to me, I guess," Julia said, and Betsy said not to worry, she had other games, and she brought out balloons and a stack of cloth diapers.

Sharon stared down at her balloon while the others hunched over theirs and tried to carefully pin on the diapers. Every time a balloon exploded, she cringed and covered her ears. "I'm going out for a smoke," she announced, and she left the room, and soon everyone abandoned the game.

Betsy leaned over to whisper to Julia. "Why did you invite her? I thought you hated Sharon?"

Julia had never hated Sharon. That first summer at Luigi's, they had been inseparable. Work and then out to the bar, their shirt sleeves rolled, their waitress aprons off. For Julia, it was a seamless, dreamy time, Robert busy writing his dissertation and teaching, Julia spending all her time with Sharon, who was six years younger, so freckled and pale, she reminded Julia of a girl in a Wyeth painting.

They'd walk home together through throngs of students. Sharon would tell Julia how she had learned to see negative space in a film course, how she hadn't really understood it before, but it was all she saw now—great odd shapes between buildings and tree branches, the city made up of Hitchcock stills. "It's like everything is reversed," she said one night. She squinted at a row of lit storefronts, dark alleys between. "You should try it. It will freak you out. It's just a habit of seeing. Once you do it, nothing will ever look the same."

Julia squinted and what she saw then was the world moving on without her, the street already a street from her past. She was a waitress with an unused degree, about to settle down and buy a house, and the thought filled her with a dreadful kind of pleasure. She was fleeing the East Coast and all her former ambitions, and, yes, she knew even then, planning to disappear in the most ordinary way.

The guests gathered at the buffet to fill their plates for lunch, and Julia gazed around at framed posters of sunflowers, photographs of Betsy and her husband on a river cruise. Betsy was easy, the kind of friend who could organize play dates, who went to yoga three times a week, who had never wanted to leave home. She hated that Sharon spoke so disparagingly of the Midwest.

As if Sharon knew Julia were thinking of her, she stepped closer, her hands wrapped around a glass of punch, her mouth ready with a quip. "You should come to a baby shower back home. Much better. Everyone brings faux food."

"We've got that here too. Rick brought fruit pizza."

"That's for amateurs," Sharon said. "Back home we make apple pie out of Ritz crackers. No apples."

"Sounds delicious," Julia said. She pulled a chair out and sat down and let herself relax.

"Yes, but nowhere near as good as Twinkie dogs," Sharon said. She was on a roll. "You just cut a Twinkie in half and then stick a Chic-o-stick inside and squirt some red and yellow frosting on top. Just like a hot dog, only better."

The baby kicked and quieted. Across the room, Sloane and Claire were suddenly getting along, trading pregnancy stories. Their voices lowered and Julia pretended she wasn't listening.

Sloane said, "We'll see who's smiling in a few months. Bet she can't fake her way through this."

Sharon had overheard as well. "Don't let them get to you," she said.

"She's probably right," Julia said. "When do you leave?"

"Soon," Sharon said. "The EU has all these rules. It's not as easy being an American as it used to be."

"You make it sound like you've been traveling for years," Julia said, suddenly annoyed.

"It's just you used to be able to fly with an open-ended ticket," Sharon said. "Now that's a red flag."

"Damn terrorists," Julia said. "They ruin everything."

Sharon stared at Julia.

"It was a joke, Sharon."

"I know, Julia." She smiled weakly, turned her cup in her hands. "Luigi misses you."

"I bet he's upset you're leaving again," Julia said.

"Are you kidding? He can't wait until I go."

Sharon had been a terrible waitress. She used to comp drinks and halve bills and check on diners every few minutes, apologizing for the slightest delays. "Slow down," Julia would tell her. "It's not fast food. Don't hover."

Her words were lost on Sharon who had never frequented restaurants herself. She hoisted trays and cleared tables in a frenzy. She injured herself on the heat lamp, spilled sauce down the front of her blouse. At least once a month, she lost her night's tips—in the back of a cab, in a bar, while walking home. There were issues with ex-boyfriends, with a teenage sister who was pregnant, with a brother who had done three tours in Iraq and Afghanistan, with her recovering alcoholic mother and her born again and again stepfather. Though she'd never met them, Julia used to do all their voices, all she needed was a prompt from Sharon.

"Look, waiting tables is a performance," Julia would say. "If you don't know about the wine, just bullshit. If it's a red, say it's leggy with notes of pepper and blackberry jam. If it's a white, mention oak barrels and hints of pear. Trust me, if they're asking, they know nothing. Just make it up."

But Sharon's delivery was awkward and overbaked. She

frightened people with her anxious voice and her over-wide eyes. She kept trying though. Just as Julia kept pretending she and Robert would eventually move to New York or LA, that Julia would start auditioning again. She told Sharon she needed help with her acting, and they watched movies together and rehearsed entire scenes. Sharon had an amazing, almost photographic memory. They started to converse in movie lines, and before long Julia could barely keep up.

Betsy set a tray of numbered diapers on the coffee table and said, "OK, everyone. This one is going to be really fun."

Sloane and Claire pretended not to hear. The other teachers looked up and then resumed their talking.

"Nobody wants to play?" Betsy said. "I've got all these prizes still."

The diapers contained some kind of unrecognizable food in shades of brown, and Sharon pulled Julia away. "Twenty bucks one of them contains Tootsie Rolls," she said. "Whoever came up with this game? It's enough to put you off kids forever."

Julia made her voice growly like Richard Burton. "All I said was that our son... the apple of our three eyes, Martha being a Cyclops... our son is a beanbag, and you get testy!"

"Look, sweetheart," Sharon said, her voice deadpan. "I can drink you under any godddamn table you want, so don't you worry about me."

Sloane looked over at the two of them worriedly, and Julia

laughed out loud, partly to reassure her sister, and partly because at that moment Sharon looked more like Sissy Spacek in *Carrie* than Liz Taylor in *Who's Afraid of Virginia Woolf.*

One night, when Luigi's was slow, Julia and Sharon got off work early and ran down the street to Frankie's piano bar. Julia hadn't seen Sharon for several days because Sharon had had some trouble back home. She had been quiet all evening. They ran out into the night air, their strides opening, their skirts flying. Frankie's was their secret spot. Not many college kids went there. It was dark and hadn't been remodeled since the 70s, and Frankie, the owner, would sit at the piano and croon.

Julia threw open the door, making a grand entrance, and she and Sharon ordered two sidecars from their favorite bartender, an English guy named Nigel.

"Hey, where's Frankie?" Julia said, taking a stool next to her. "No piano tonight?"

"All yours, beautiful," Nigel said. He set the drinks in front of them.

"Come on, drink up," Julia said to Sharon. "You act like someone just died."

"Someone just did," Sharon said, and she told Julia how her stepfather had been sleeping with her mother's sister, how her uncle had shot them, killing her aunt and wounding her stepfather. Then, her uncle had driven down a county road and fatally shot himself.

"Jesus. Why didn't you tell me?" Julia said.

"I am telling you. I'm telling you now," Sharon said.

Her mother had been working at the time. "She thinks it's her fault. That she drove them all to it or something." Her stepfather was in the ICU, and Sharon had been at the hospital, keeping vigil with her mother.

"I'm so sorry," Julia said. She didn't know what else to say.

Sharon stared moodily down at her drink. She told Julia how the entire town knew everything now, how her mother didn't want to return home. "It's like something you'd hear on *Jerry Springer*," she said. "Please don't tell anyone."

Nigel rapped on the bar in front of Julia. "Play that one song for me, love. You know the one."

The bar was filled with people they didn't know. Julia turned to look at the piano on the small stage behind them, the empty tip jar, the light filtering down.

"You might as well go ahead," Sharon said.

"I'll cheer you up," Julia said, but she just wanted to cheer herself. The summer was ending, and she and Robert were arguing about money and whether to start a family, about the possibility of staying in Michigan for good. Julia played show tunes and sang, imagining she was playing the part of a washed-up actress-cum-waitress in a cheesy Midwestern bar. She husked her voice and directed her eyes at an old man, wagging a finger at him. Nigel poured her drinks on the house. "You should be famous, love," he said, and they slipped into the alley to smoke a joint with Sharon. After Nigel went back inside, Julia sidled closer to Sharon. "Everything is going to be OK," she said, and Sharon said, "No it's not, Julia. Everything has changed."

Inside, someone was playing the opening bars of "Fly Me to the Moon."

"Hey, that's my song," Julia said, and she pulled Sharon back into Frankie's and let go of her hand. She drank until the place was spinning and empty and dark, until Nigel was stacking the stools on the bar and Sharon was standing by the door with their purses.

Julia stumbled outside and threw up. "What am I doing here?" she said to Sharon, and she didn't know if she meant the town or the bar. She sat down on the curb, and the street was ugly, the night too warm.

Sharon took Julia to her studio apartment and tucked her into her pullout bed. She called Julia's husband to explain that Julia had gotten so drunk she'd be sleeping over. All night, she helped Julia to the bathroom to throw up, and in the morning, she sat in bed with Julia and read aloud a *National Geographic* article about some ritualistic tribe that forced sticks through their skin and then spontaneously healed.

Julia was still nauseous and had a headache. Robert had a dinner she was expected to attend later that day. She remembered Sharon's stepfather and asked her if she had any more news.

"I'm getting out of here, Julia. I hate this place."

"When did running away ever solve anything?" she said.

"You ran away."

"I moved. I got married. It's different."

"Sure," Sharon said. "Whatever you say."

Betsy was arranging bowls of baby food and spoons on the coffee table. "I'm sensing a theme," Julia said to Sharon.

"Come on, everyone," Betsy said. "This is the last one. I promise. Winner has to guess all six. Remember, if you say the word *baby* you lose a point."

"You just said it," Rick said, and Betsy said, "Oh my God, I did." She took her pencil and deducted a point from the running score she was keeping on a piece of paper.

Betsy had gone to great lengths to plan the perfect party, even fashioning napkin rings out of pacifiers. "Sharon," she said. "Stop hogging Julia. You go first."

"Just pretend you're an anthropologist from the future," Julia whispered.

Sharon picked up a plastic spoon and dipped it into the first bowl. "Sweet potatoes?" she said. "Do I have to taste them all?"

A few weeks after that night at Frankie's, Julia had been on her way to meet Robert for lunch when she saw Sharon go into the university art museum. It took Julia several minutes of wandering around the building before she found Sharon sitting on a bench before a stark abstract painting. Julia was so arrested by Sharon's open stare, by the downward pull of her mouth that she simply sat beside her. Neither of them talked for some moments, and then Sharon said, "When you look at that blue square, do you feel like it's coming at you or moving away?"

Julia stared at the painting. She'd never been a fan of abstracts. The painting reminded her of farmland and was divided into swaths of green, yellow, and red, with the rectangle of blue just off-center. "I don't know," she said. "I don't feel anything." But the more she stared at the piece, the more uncomfortable she became. The painting turned inside out and back again. Just when she thought she had a hold on a horizon, it slipped away.

She had already begun spending time with Betsy by then. With Betsy, Julia could spend long hours shopping or sharing advice about marriage and careers. Betsy loved comedies and Michigan football. When Julia joked around, Betsy never looked into the dark spaces between her words, she just laughed.

They had abandoned the game and were now digging into second servings of food. Paper plates lay stacked next to the diapers and bowls. Sloane and Betsy were relaxed and a little drunk and sank deep into the couch. The teachers circled around them on wooden chairs pulled from the dining table. Even Sharon looked at ease, sitting cross-legged on the floor, her shoes off, a spot of frosting on her black dress.

The clothesline of baby clothes hung so low they had to duck to leave the room. "We should dance the Limbo," Julia said.

"Let's not and say we did," Rick said. He told a story about Julia, how he had walked into her classroom to find the entire class pretending to be birds. "She can make them do anything," he said. "Seventh graders too. You should have heard all of them squawking."

"That doesn't surprise me," Sloane said. She told stories about their childhood, how they had lived in costumes, how they had turned the backyard into a theater. Julia sat beside Betsy and only half listened. She was thinking about the baby, wondering if she would take after her or Robert or be unlike both of them. She looked around the room at her friends and imagined barbecues and birthday parties. Sharon would miss out. There would be school pageants, weekend camping trips, graduations. Her daughter would grow older. She would pull away and eventually leave home.

"What were you just thinking about?" Sloane asked.

Everyone turned to look at Julia, especially Sharon, who studied her face as if it were one of her paintings. "Is there any more of that fruit pizza?" Julia said, recovering herself. "Sharon just loves it. And cake. Let us eat cake!"

To think that Julia had dreaded running into Sharon all summer. Then in August she bumped into her coming out of a shop downtown. Julia hadn't recognized her at first because Sharon had cut her hair and was wearing a severe skirt and button-down shirt. As she walked toward Julia, it was as if an older, tougher woman had taken residence in Sharon. Julia had been a little disoriented at first, but then Sharon pointed to Julia's stomach and said, "When did that happen?"

"I've got two and a half more months yet. Can you believe it?"

They were standing at the corner, Julia smiling too forcefully, pretending they had parted on friendlier terms, that it hadn't been so long since they'd last seen each other. "I didn't know you were back in town," Julia lied.

They walked together, and Sharon carried Julia's bags for her and told her a story about mothers in Germany and how a woman once left her baby stroller in the middle of the sidewalk to chase Sharon and scold her for cutting across the train tracks. Sharon tried to imitate the woman's voice, saying, "You there, Fraulein. What are you doing then? It is against the rules." It was a horrible impersonation that sounded vaguely Russian. "It's been so long. I missed you, Julia," she said.

She was still the old Sharon after all, trying too hard, overly sincere.

"We should get coffee sometime," Julia said, reaching for her bags to be on her way.

"How about now?" Sharon said. They were standing in front of a new patisserie, and Julia was caught off guard. She said, "OK. But I've only got a few minutes."

Inside, Sharon swirled cream into her coffee and sipped. She had been sneaking into art history lectures at the university in Berlin. She told Julia about an artist who commissioned a life-size doll of his ex-lover and paraded her through the streets after World War I. "Everyone thinks the war made him crazy, but I don't think so. I think he was just putting on a show. Creating a stir."

"What happened to him?"

"I don't know. I think he wound up in Switzerland. He taught in Minnesota for a while."

"Maybe it really was the war. Maybe he wasn't pretending. People do change, Sharon. You, of all people, should know that."

"How's your mother?" Julia asked. What she really wanted to know is whether her mother was still with Sharon's awful stepfather. About a month after the shooting, he had limped into Luigi's with a cane, a heavyset man with broad shoulders and long, unruly hair. The kind of man that might have once been a catch in a small, dying town. He handed Sharon an envelope that she tucked into her apron pocket. Then he wrapped his arm around her waist and whispered something that caused Sharon's lips to curl in disgust.

After he left, Julia had asked, "Was that him? What did he want?"

"Nothing," Sharon said. "This isn't one of your dramas, Julia."

A couple of women were standing at the door, waiting to be seated. It was Julia's turn, but Sharon sat them in her own section. She had become so ambitious, so bent on leaving the country that the others hated working with her. Though her serving skills hadn't improved much, she smiled at customers now. She flirted and talked them into more expensive meals and bottles of wine. Instead of going out after work, she hoarded her tips. Little by little, she and Julia drifted apart.

At the café, Sharon explained that her mother was doing better and that she had missed her while she was away. She had been working at a Turkish restaurant in Berlin, but without a visa. She had a lover waiting for her too. "I think it's serious," she said, but something in her eyes said she wasn't sure. There was still a cloud around Sharon, a gloominess that reached with little tendrils, and Julia covered her belly with her hands and said, "I've got to get home. Robert will be worried."

Sharon responded with a slight smile, as if she knew Julia wanted nothing more to do with her, and suddenly Julia wanted to prove her wrong. "You remember Betsy?" she said. "She's throwing me a shower. You should come."

Michiganders had such a hard time saying goodbye. Julia had opened gift after gift, and now everyone lingered near the door. Betsy and Julia ushered the teachers and Sharon outside. The teachers lingered before their cars joking and talking about the coming school year. Julia couldn't believe it was almost fall. You could smell it in the air.

Across the street, Betsy's neighbors had planted a giant pumpkin patch in their front yard, and green pumpkins grew in a monstrous tangle of vines.

Sharon followed Julia's eyes. "They're like huge seed pods!" she said, reading Julia's mind.

"We had to dig him out from under the most peculiar things," Julia said.

Betsy looked at them queerly. "Don't tell me. Another movie?"

Julia gave Sharon a hug and said, "It was really good to see you. We need to get together again before you leave." This time she meant it, but Sharon said, "I don't think I'll have time, but I'll call you when I'm back in the States. And, wow, you'll be a mom." She made her way down the walk to the road, waving goodbye to Rick, who was pulling away in his car.

"How did she get here?" Betsy said. "She couldn't have walked."

"I don't know," Julia said. "Can you get a bus out here?"

"Yes, but she'll have to walk a while. Why didn't she ask someone for a ride?"

Sloane was still in the house. "Come on," Julia said to Betsy. She held the door open, but before following Betsy inside, she turned to look one last time. In her black dress, Sharon was a dark cutout in the landscape, getting smaller. Julia squinted to see the negative space between them, to blur the fields, the road, the rows of townhouses.

"Julia!" Betsy called.

Julia went inside and closed the door behind her. Whether she was emerging or being swallowed depended on a trick of the eye. A person could be two things at once. In the living room, Betsy and her sister had flung themselves on the couch and were eating the last of the cake. "What were you doing out there?" they said, and they welcomed her like she'd been gone for days.

HOW TO WALK ON WATER

I'LL SHOW YOU THE BACKSIDE OF YOUR SOUL. THAT'S WHAT Arvel Wilkes told Nolan's mother, Sigrid, the night of the attack. Nolan had found a manila envelope with a smeared carbon copy of the original police report inside. Sigrid had been just twenty-six when it happened, younger than Nolan now. The report didn't note what his mother said in response to Wilkes, just that there were "minimal defensive marks on victim." They had been living on the north side of Seattle at the time, his father away on a business trip, Nolan asleep in his crib.

He was home to pull his life together, staying in his mother's guest room, trying to keep out of her way. She couldn't fall asleep without the radio. She left her bedroom door ajar for her cat, and Nolan crept closer to listen. *Was Princess Diana's death a setup? What about JFK Jr.? We're going to hear from a man who claims there is a secret profession of accident staging. Later in the hour, I'll be opening the call lines. Do you believe in evil? What led you, or someone you know, to a moment of evil?*

"Too loud?" Sigrid said. She must have sensed Nolan standing outside the door. "I can turn it off."

"I thought you called me," he said. She tuned in to the same station every night. Aliens. The supernatural. Government conspiracies. Time travel. It wasn't like his mother to listen to such things. "I'm going to bed now," he said. "I'll make sure the doors are locked."

He went into the guest room and shut the door. His mother's desk was there, her photo albums, her boxes of tax and financial records. He'd found the envelope, along with a recent letter from the Seattle Police Department, while rifling through the desk for her checkbook. Arvel Wilkes had died in prison. She hadn't mentioned it.

Nolan called his father in Pensacola and told him he'd been hunting for information, that he found a medical report and knew Sigrid could never have another child. "Is that why you divorced?" he asked. "Is that why she never dated anyone?"

His father still loved Sigrid. It hadn't been his idea to separate, and Nolan suspected he'd finally left and remarried because there was no going back to the way it had been. "You always liked to pick at scabs," his father said now. "Never could leave well enough alone."

"Dad, I'm worried about Mom. She's into all this UFO and shadow government shit. She's losing it."

"She never says nothing to me about UFOs. I talked to her the other day. She's worried about you. She said you just sit around on your ass all day. She thinks you're depressed."

"So you and Mom didn't split up because of what happened?"

Nolan could hear his father rattle ice in a glass, looking for the perfect cube to chomp. "Your mother and I are OK," he said, biting down. "We're just different people, that's all. She met someone she could talk to back then. She couldn't talk to me."

"Who?"

"That was a long time ago. Don't bring up Wilkes with her. You let that monster rot."

"How did the job search go today?" Sigrid asked. She filled a watering can and fussed over a plant on the table where Nolan was paging through a newspaper. Somehow the day had gotten away from him, and he still hadn't showered or shaved.

"Nothing yet," Nolan said. "I'll find something."

Over the past few years, he had lived in towns all over Colorado and Wyoming, working as a bartender, a rental manager, a warehouse supervisor, and a short-order cook. He had borrowed money from Sigrid to build his own food truck, but that project never quite got off the ground. His most recent venture was with his ex-girlfriend, Brenda. That winter they'd paid for rent and ski passes with insurance payments for a bogus accident. When the money ran out, they called college kids about bank errors, trying to get their usernames and passwords to drain their accounts. They managed to get ahold of one unsuspecting girl's password, but when they logged in to her account, the girl had just $92. "Well," Brenda said, "At least we know how to do it now. That's a start." But for Nolan it was the end.

He was almost thirty and tired of dead-end jobs, of falling in and out of love. He waited for Brenda to go out and called his mother to ask if he could come home. It had been two and a half years since he'd seen her. To his relief, Sigrid hadn't asked many questions. She just said she'd had a feeling he would call, and then she wired him money for airfare.

She sat down now with a cup of hot water and a slice of

lemon. "You should call some of your old friends from high school."

He glanced up from the paper and stared. They'd been through this all before.

"Well, there's got to be someone," she said. She was semi-retired and worked part-time for the city clerk, even volunteered at a literacy center downtown. She brought home university extension catalogs and left them on the table for him. "It wouldn't take much, Nolan," she'd say. "Just five or six more courses."

She was about to start in on him again. He had gone to college in Boulder on a diving scholarship but dropped out after a few years. He didn't want to hear it. On the refrigerator, she had a magnet that read *Talk is Cheap*. He couldn't mention Wilkes to her, but she could listen to harrowing stories on the radio all night long.

"Why do you listen to that show?" he said. "You don't believe that shit, do you?"

"What show?" She was taken off guard, and then she laughed. "Oh, you mean my radio program?" She twisted the lemon and dropped it into the cup. "It's quite entertaining, really. Better than those political ones. I can't stand those."

"And you don't get nightmares listening to alien stories?"

"See," she said. "You can't help listening either." She studied him. "It's funny having you here. I feel like I need to get to know you all over again." She stood and opened a cupboard and looked inside. "Do you still like the curly noodles? I bought some for you. Remember how you wouldn't eat spaghetti? I couldn't convince you it was made out of the same ingredients."

He folded the newspaper over, snapped it to let her know he was trying to read. He'd scanned the paper in five minutes that morning, and now he read the same article about a missing child that had been found in Oregon and brought back to his family in Minnesota.

"When you get an interview, you'll have to wear a button-down and cover those tattoos." She wanted to know if he regretted getting them now.

"No, Mother. I like them."

"Really? Even that cartoon one? Remember how you hid it from me?"

When he was eighteen he'd had the Tasmanian Devil inked on his forearm. He thought it would make him appear both tough and funny. It looked more like a bloated squirrel, not that he'd ever admit this to Sigrid. She worried about his pierced ears, too. "They look like bolts, Nolan. Like Frankenstein. That can't be sanitary. You'll stretch them out. Someday that won't be in style, and then what will you do?"

He stared at the thin scar jagging up her cheek and across her temple. It was barely perceptible now, and she didn't even bother trying to hide it. "I'm sure I'll be fine," he said. "It's just skin."

"Oh, I know," she said. "But you know how people can be."

You know me, Wilkes had said to his victims, and he meant it literally. He'd worked at the neighborhood grocery store as a bagger. He'd held crying babies while mothers loaded their carts, chatted with husbands waiting outside in their cars. No one suspected him, not at first. Sure, his coworkers wondered why he didn't have a better job, why at forty-three he still lived with his mother. They all agreed there was something "off" about Wilkes, but he seemed friendly enough.

Sigrid had other scars too, on her legs, on her torso. When Nolan was growing up, she'd told him they were from an incident when he was a baby. He had always thought she'd gotten into a car accident, and not even his father had told him the real story until he was in high school. "Your mother didn't want to burden you, that's why," his father said when Nolan asked him why they had lied. "She white-knuckled it for years. For you, kid."

Nolan shut the door of his room and pretended to search for jobs on Sigrid's slow desktop computer. He pushed his suitcase up against the door and pulled out the report. Somewhere in a police department basement were the originals. He imagined his mother in a hospital bed, two detectives pressing her for details. His father had told him that much, that they played good cop, bad cop, that they made her tell her story over and over. His father had thrown a fit and almost landed in jail.

The detectives must have asked Sigrid to list everything Wilkes said and did. *You're not very pretty, but I will show you your soul. It is a sneaky thing. We will have to work very hard to get it all.* Nolan knew his mother. She'd lived in Seattle most of her adult life, but she was still a stoic Midwesterner at heart. She would have reported just a few of the things Wilkes said, leaving out the worst details. She couldn't stand anything lurid. She hated emotional displays.

That night she had left Nolan with a babysitter and gone

to the Oasis tavern, where Wilkes was drinking. She'd told the police he must have followed her home, but there was some question of whether she might have accepted a ride, whether he had waited outside for the babysitter to leave. There was no sign of forced entry. Sigrid told the officers she might have forgotten to lock the door. They knew Wilkes's profile, knew his victim type: petite, new mother, what they later described as a "reluctant Madonna type." By then they had gathered a list of women who had disappeared from the area, but they had only circumstantial evidence linking them to Wilkes, and no bodies, yet.

When Sigrid was out during the day, Nolan watched TV and took long baths. He stole twenties from a soapbox his mother hid in her dresser and felt like a teenager again. He had no money, just what little she gave him for spending. In his suitcase, he had two blank checks from her desk. He just needed a few weeks to clear his head. If things worked out, he'd tear them up and she'd never know. If not, he'd cash them on the way out of town. He kept a six-pack of cheap beer in the refrigerator and replaced what he drank before Sigrid returned in the evening. One afternoon, he tried to recreate the aftermath of the attack by pulling himself out of the tub and crawling across the tile. He hadn't gotten very far. He only managed to scrape his knees and scare the cat.

When Sigrid came home, she said, "What's this water all over the floor? Did you spill something?" He told her he had taken a bath and forgotten his towel, and she had looked at him queerly and said, "There's a shower right next to your room."

In *The Seattle Times* online archives, Nolan found an article

from when Wilkes was put away for Sigrid's assault and rape in
'84. In the picture, his face was boyish, his blond hair thinning,
and he had dull, close-set eyes. If Nolan had passed Wilkes on
the sidewalk, he would have never given him a second glance.
They had failed to get Wilkes on attempted murder. He was
out on parole eight years later, lived just hours from Sigrid for
twenty more years, until he was finally convicted of the murder
and dismemberment of a young woman in Coeur d'Alene, Idaho.
He'd confessed to killing six others, though investigators believed
there were many more. Nolan was in Colorado when he heard
the news and called his mother. She told him detectives had been
visiting her for years, trying to put Wilkes away. She'd said this
like it was just another piece of passing news.

At the pool, Nolan changed into the new trunks Sigrid had
bought him and took a shower. When he looked in the mirror,
he didn't recognize the man staring back. He had a paunch. His
chest was a little sunken, his tattoos faded from years in the sun.
His shoulders were no longer the shoulders of a swimmer. He
walked along the edge of the pool, past a children's swimming
class to the lanes reserved for laps.

   He didn't have goggles, and the chlorine stung his eyes, but
he was surprised how quickly the strokes came back, how his
arms and legs remembered, how his breath fell into a rhythm,
how he simply turned into the next lap. He heard his coach's
voice in his ear. "No resistance, Nolan. Don't think. Just swim."
He couldn't get that lightness though. He felt himself straining,

fighting the water, allowing his arms and legs to create a drag, to chop instead of slice. He hung onto the edge of the pool to catch his breath.

When Nolan was five he'd tried to walk on water. Sigrid had been trying out religions then. She took Nolan to a Catholic Mass, and afterward Nolan joined the kids in the church basement, where they colored pictures of Peter walking on water toward Jesus. One of the sisters explained that a sudden wind had frightened Peter and he lost his faith and started to sink. She asked the children, "Do you believe?" and all the children nodded, and Nolan believed too.

He had gone to the beach at Golden Gardens with family friends a few weeks later. He led another boy down to the marina and walked to the end of a dock, sailboats moored all around. He said, "Watch," and then he stepped off the pier, thinking of Jesus, and he was genuinely shocked when his feet slipped through the surface and he was underwater, thrashing, his ears pounding, his lungs seizing. A man jumped in after him and lifted him onto the dock. He hadn't been there, and then he was. The next day, Sigrid signed Nolan up for swimming lessons, and the rest of that summer she forced him into the water over and over until he was too tired to cry.

The man in the next lane moved slowly, crashing forward, kicking up huge waves. A woman swam against his wake, and she stopped now and then to recover before starting again. The diving board gave Nolan a feeling of vertigo, but he couldn't stop looking up at it. He hadn't dived in years, not since training for the conference championship when he was a junior in college and botched his first dive, only to blow out an eardrum on the second. His ear healed, but he gave up. He didn't even formally quit. He just left school and never returned for his senior year. His father was furious, but Sigrid told him he could always come back home and finish school there. "There are worse things," she said.

The man in the other lane looked satisfied as he pulled himself out of the water and his feet slapped the wet tile, thrilled that he had finished however many laps he had set for himself that day. On the other side of the pool, toddlers were getting lessons, and Nolan thought of Sigrid jumping in with him for his own first lessons, though she couldn't swim herself. He still remembered her scars when he opened his eyes and tried to dive around her, how they wove up her legs, raised and thick as vines.

Sometimes Nolan talked to Wilkes in his head. *Why'd you do it, you miserable fuck?* Sometimes Wilkes answered him in a nasally voice that sounded from a distance. *I'm upside down. Do you see me up here in the corner?* That's what he'd said to Sigrid when she was lying in the tub, passing in and out of consciousness. She told the detectives he'd talked like he owned the voice of God.

Nolan tried to imagine Wilkes's face, to slowly obliterate it, but he kept seeing his mother instead, in a yellow dress, her hair freshly washed and smelling like strawberry shampoo, walking into the Oasis, happy to be out of the house for the night, away from her baby. According to the police report, she had gone alone but hadn't noticed or talked to Wilkes, though other witnesses placed him there sitting a few stools down. Next to Sigrid's words, the detective had scribbled a question mark and circled it.

A witness claimed that Sigrid had talked to several men that night and that she was wearing a miniskirt. In the report, the word "miniskirt" was underlined twice, as were "two brandy old-fashioneds."

After Wilkes was through with Sigrid and left her unconscious in her bathtub, he went to the hardware store for a tarp and then stopped back at the tavern before heading back. The detectives thought this was to solidify his alibi, but Nolan pictured Wilkes sipping his cold beer, a barely detectable smugness on his unremarkable face. He might have gone to the tavern to celebrate, to draw the experience out. Meanwhile, Sigrid had come to and inched out of the bathroom and all the way out the door. A neighbor found her on the front lawn, unconscious, wearing nothing but a bloody towel. Nolan had slept through it all.

He folded the report and slipped it into the manila folder and closed the flap, wrapping the dry, brown string around the clasp.

He had moved a second radio into his room and turned it down low. People called in from all over the country. Truckers told tales of haunted rigs and ghost dogs in the road in the middle of the night, and he could hear the highway around their husked voices, see them sleeping in their cabs at rest stops. Others called about the feeling of *déjà vu* right before a calamitous event, or about seeing loved ones moments after they died.

He turned the radio down and heard the same muffled voices coming from his mother's room. The harder he listened the more he heard a split-second delay between them, and he lay awake trying to blend the sounds together again, trying not to hear an echo.

They were having lunch at the kitchen table, eating cucumbers on rye with tomato soup, and Sigrid handed Nolan a napkin. It amazed him how little she ate. She looked like a grandmother now, her eyes smaller, nearly lost in lines. She wore long skirts and round-necked sweaters and flat European shoes. She had matured into her name, into her condo with its blue and white teacups.

She set her sandwich down on her plate. "I don't want you around here all day, brooding. It's making me crazy."

"Why? You're not even here most of the time."

He wanted a burger. She used too much butter. Thick slabs of butter. She had very little in her refrigerator, but she had plenty of butter. Nolan stood and tossed his uneaten sandwich into the garbage. He grabbed a beer and popped it open, watched Sigrid ignore its slow hiss.

"Life goes fast, Nolan. It's the things you don't do that you'll regret."

"Really?" he said. "I wonder what Arvel Wilkes would say about that. You let him in. Didn't you, Mom?"

She folded her napkin and dropped it on her plate. "You've

been going through my things again. I want you to stay out of my papers. I don't know what you think you'll find."

"You probably offered him a sandwich. With butter. Lots of butter."

"You're just trying to upset me," she said. She stood and rinsed her plate and put it in the dishwasher. "Why are you being so ugly lately? Why did you come back here if you hate me so much? What is it you want?"

"Nothing, Mom."

"Well, obviously, it's not nothing." Her back was to him. She didn't turn around. She bent down to pull a bucket out from under the sink. "Get out of the kitchen. I'm going to scrub the floor."

"Mom," he said. "I'm sorry. Jesus. I'm sorry. OK?"

She filled the bucket in the sink. "I don't know what it is that makes you want to hurt me. I don't know what I did. But you have no right. Not about him. Not about that."

Nolan nudged the radio closer. He gasped out loud when a caller mentioned seeing a purple disc of light above the mountains in Santa Fe. When a woman called to say she went hiking and returned to the parking lot to discover that she'd been gone for three days and could only remember a flash in the sky, a metal table and probing instruments, Nolan surprised himself by uttering a faint, shocked, "No way." He supposed something similar had happened to him. A flash and years gone by, and he had nothing to show for it, not really, not even a pot to piss in, as his father would say.

Late the next morning, Sigrid opened the blinds by the bed and said, "I'm beginning to think your father was right. I'm doing you a real disservice letting you stay here."

"I'm getting up, Mom." He turned over and burrowed into the pillow.

Sigrid stood at the end of the bed. "Did you take my checks? I'm missing two checks and I want to know if you stole them, Nolan."

"What are you talking about?" he said. He sat up in the bed and looked her straight in the eyes. "I don't have your stupid checks. Maybe you forgot to write them down."

"You're going out today, and I'm going to lock the door. I don't care what you do, but you're not staying here. I want you to give me your key."

He sat up. "You've got to be kidding. I'm not a child, mother."

"Tell me about it," she said. "I'm calling the bank today, too."

After he dressed and stuffed the blank checks into his pocket, he hopped a bus to Belltown to wait with the day laborers for work. Every city had a corner like this one. People would pull up in their trucks and SUVs with odd jobs, and men would clamor about, arguing over whose turn it was next. Nolan tried to get the jobs requiring two or more workers. He didn't like going to someone's house alone. Once, in Denver, he went with a man to his mansion in the suburbs to shovel truckloads of gravel onto a long driveway. The man told him he'd pay twenty an hour, but at the end of a full day he gave Nolan fifty bucks. Nolan had nearly pummeled the guy. He was left without a way home, but he took the fifty dollars and threw it on the ground and said, "You need this more than I do." It wasn't true. That night he went out to a bar and got into a fight with a guy more down on his luck than Nolan, and by the next morning he was facing a five-hundred-dollar fine and community service.

He'd been waiting for over an hour, standing back from the other men, feeling the draw of the clean paper checks in his back pocket. He'd find someplace to cash them and get out of town. Leave his suitcase at his mother's. She had plenty of money. She'd be fine. Then a young couple pulled up. It was just a few hours of work, helping them move. He hopped into the truck with a tiny Ecuadorian guy named Rolando, and they drove up to a house on Phinney Ridge and hauled furniture and supermarket boxes filled with books into a rental van. Rolando lifted two boxes for every one of Nolan's, and Nolan worked harder. Sweat poured down his back. Not everything would fit in the truck, and the couple started arguing. Finally the woman paid them and said they might as well go.

Sigrid had called and left a message on his cell phone, telling him she was going to grill steaks that night, but Nolan didn't want to go home. He felt itchy and wild, and he and Rolando walked downhill to a bar in Fremont filled with college kids and hipsters. The beers were six dollars a pint, too much for Rolando. "Come on, man," Nolan said. "Let me buy you one." Rolando looked around warily, and Nolan couldn't convince him to stay. Nolan drank one pint while pretending to watch a soccer game on TV. A girl in a sundress stood next to him, her arms inked in colorful, intricate designs, and he watched her until she turned around. "I like your tats," he said, and she looked frightened and slid deeper into the crowd. He needed a shower. His shirt was striped with sweat and dirt. He set his empty glass down on the bar and slipped outside to wait for the next bus home.

It was almost dark by the time he reached the condo, but Sigrid grilled his steak on the patio in her pajamas and robe. He could tell she felt bad about accusing him, about making him leave for the day. She placed a cold beer next to his plate and sat down to watch him eat. The work and the walking had given him an appetite, and he knew she was waiting for him to tell her how good the steak was, to tell her about his day.

"You were always so good-natured, Nolan. What happened? Why are you so angry? Did something happen to you?"

"I'm not angry, Mom. I'm fine."

Sigrid hugged herself against the chill. "It's not good to keep everything bottled up."

"You ought to know."

"You're just itching for a fight. Your father called. He's worried about you."

"Everybody's worried," Nolan said, but he was too tired to keep arguing. The last of the sun slipped behind the ridge, and they went inside, and Nolan washed the dishes while his mother got ready for bed.

In the envelope with the police report, Nolan had found a dried wildflower and a handwritten message on police notepaper. *We'll make it, Sig, if we stick together.* Maybe Sigrid had fallen for one of the cops that questioned her. Maybe this was the man his father meant, the one she talked to when she couldn't talk to him.

Maybe the good cop said, "You're lucky to be alive."

"Luck," the bad cop grunted. "You call that lucky?"

His mother would have preferred the bad cop. When she finally spoke the words Wilkes said to her, it would have been to him.

The bad cop didn't try to comfort. He let her see the crime scene photos, though it was against rules. He would never have said, "It wasn't your fault. You couldn't have fought back." He suspected they'd find others buried somewhere. "Life is shit," he would have said. "Luck is staying alive."

Sigrid was asleep when Nolan left the house again. He could hear her radio as he snatched her car keys from the hook on the kitchen wall. He drove to Aurora Avenue, looking for the tavern where his mother had met Wilkes. The street was still lined with greasy diners and Chinese restaurants, seedy motels with vintage neon signs. *Free Local Calls. $45 a night. Vacancy.* The Oasis still existed, squeezed between a tire shop and the run-down Rosebud Inn with its painted sign bleached to pink and weeds sprouting from the lot where he parked.

Inside the tavern, dusty luau flowers covered the ceiling. On a small stage at the back of the room was a plastic palm tree wrapped with a string of lights. Nolan pulled out a stool and sat down at the bar. The bartender was an older woman with penciled eyebrows. She slapped a cardboard coaster in front of Nolan and said, "I got Anchor Steam. Two-dollar special tonight."

There were two others, a man and a woman, at the bar drinking schooners, and Nolan nodded and said, "Sure." They all stared up at the television. The Mariners were up by two, but Oakland sent up their best hitter, and soon the game was tied.

The bartender stood talking to the woman at the end of the bar. She had a smoker's mouth, and when she laughed it sounded like she'd swallowed something with claws. She stepped outside to have a cigarette, told them to shout if they needed anything. The man sitting two stools down from Nolan still slicked back his hair like it was 1957. His face was pockmarked. His shirtsleeves, rolled. He pulled a pack of cigarettes from his front pocket, snapped open the lid and closed it again. "Still weird to not be able to smoke in bars," he said to Nolan. He looked back up at the TV. The A's scored again. "Crap," he said. "There goes that."

Nolan didn't know what he had expected. You couldn't go back in time. You couldn't really imagine, and why did he want to when his mother was all right now, when Wilkes was dead, when Nolan didn't have a single memory of any of it.

The man with the slicked-back hair wanted to buy a shot for Nolan and the woman at the end of the bar.

"OK," the woman said. "Why not. Make mine a raspberry kamikaze."

"Maureen," the bartender said. "You better not be driving home tonight."

"You know I never drive on Fridays," Maureen said. She tossed back the shot and wiped her mouth. She had red, runny eyes and the look of a professional drinker. She thanked the man but didn't get too close. She leaned over to touch the bartender's arm. "Call me a cab, will you? I might as well go home."

The bartender went around to the other side of the bar and put her arm around Maureen's shoulders and squeezed. She apologized for there not being more men around. "Next week we got karaoke. You come back then, honey. We'll fix you up good."

When the taxi arrived, Maureen stumbled out the propped-open door in her red cowboy boots, and the three of them watched her get into the cab. The bartender picked up her empty glass and plunged it into the suds behind the bar.

"You been working here long?" Nolan asked.

"Too long," she said.

"How long is that?"

"Almost six years now." She slapped a rag across the bar and turned around to glance up at the clock.

Nolan tried to picture the place as his mother had known it, full of customers, someone playing guitar up on stage. "One more for the road?" he asked the man. He felt obligated to buy a round.

"Sure," the man said. "What the hell."

The bartender poured them both another whisky, and Nolan paid. He couldn't feel the alcohol yet. His stomach was too full of steak, and he couldn't get comfortable on the padded stool. He asked for a glass of water, ate another handful of peanuts from the greasy bowl in front of him.

The man looked at Nolan as he tipped back the shot. "Thank

you," he said, and then he sipped his unfinished beer. He played with the top of the cigarette pack, and his fingernails were long and yellowed and dirty, and everything in the bar seemed dirty too, and the bartender started to cough and pulled a balled-up tissue from her pocket and spat into it.

Nolan pushed himself back from the counter. "Thanks," he said to the bartender. "Take it easy," he said to the man and walked out into the cool night. If he got to sleep soon, he could get up early and make it downtown to get one of the better jobs. If that didn't work, he could sign up at a temp agency. He'd done that before.

Outside, he walked to the lot next to the motel, and Sigrid's car was gone. He went into the motel office and asked the man behind the counter about it, and the man said, "Didn't you see the sign? You can't park here if you're not a guest."

Nolan stepped under the awning of the tavern and took out his phone to call Sigrid. He'd have to wake her, and it would be like he was in high school again and in trouble, calling her because he'd wrecked the car or run out of gas or was too drunk to drive. There'd be a ticket he couldn't pay, his mother's car stuck at the impound lot.

A bus rolled down the street but didn't stop. He had probably missed the last one.

Just then, the man with the slicked-back hair left the bar. He walked like he had once been a much larger man and had lost a lot of weight.

"You all right, son?"

"Car got towed."

"Where you headed?"

"It's OK. I can walk."

"Come on. I'll give you a lift."

Nolan followed him down the street to his rusted Civic. The man said, "Just give me a sec to move some crap out of the front. Hell of a night, huh?"

There was a clear sky and a full, perfect moon. A car full of kids drove by and a long-haired girl stuck her head out the window and shouted something unintelligible.

"Somebody's having a good time," the man said. He looked up at the moon. "That kind of night. Crazies gonna come out."

Nolan tried the door, and the man said, "Sorry. Door's broken. Here, let me." He wiggled the handle until the door opened, threw a shaving kit and a stack of papers into the back and brushed some garbage onto the floor. "Hop in," he said.

The car smelled of fast food and the man's sweat. A suit was draped over a mound of laundry in the backseat. Nolan rested his feet on wrappers and empty paper cups. A rosary hung from the mirror, and underneath it on the dash was a bobble-headed dachshund.

"Where can I drop you?"

Nolan told him. "But you don't have to take me the whole way."

"I've got nowhere I need to be."

Nolan tried to make small talk, but the man drove and didn't say a word, and when Nolan finally quieted, the man said, "What do you do for a living, son?"

"Nothing right now. I just moved here. Still looking."

This seemed to make the man more interested. "That why you're all alone tonight? Ain't got no friends?"

They weren't driving that fast, maybe forty tops. The man's fingernails were too long. They were thick and ragged, and he clenched the steering wheel a little too hard. The inside handle of the passenger door was crushed in. If something went wrong, Nolan would have to throw his body against it, try to jimmy it open.

The man turned on the radio and listened. *Scientists prove precognition in animals. That's right, folks. Apparently, a parrot in Brazil has been able to predict the actions of its keeper.*

He turned the volume down. "You hear about that black bear down in Ballard?"

"No. What happened to it?"

"Made its way up north a ways. Someone spotted it in Edmonds, but then nothing. Just up and disappeared."

The car felt too cramped. The man seemed nice enough, but Nolan had an uneasy feeling. "You know what," he said. "I kind of feel like walking. It's so nice out. You can just let me off here."

"That's a long way to hoof it." The man nodded at the rosary hanging from the mirror. "You got nothing to fear from me, son, if that's what you're worried about."

Nolan laughed uncomfortably. "I think I drank too much," he said, though he was feeling all right. "I don't want to throw up in your car. It will help to walk."

"You think this car ain't been puked on before?" Now the man laughed. "I could tell you stories. Boy, could I." He reached over and patted Nolan's knee, and Nolan inched closer to the door.

"Then there was that coyote over in Discovery Park. They had to close the park down and tranquilize it. Took it up to the Cascades, but some say they seen it back again. That's the way it is, a thing's always got to come back home. You hear about the deer?"

He was heading the right direction, but in a roundabout way, taking all the narrow side streets. No people were out walking, but lights were on in apartments and houses.

"You ever listen to this show?"

"No," Nolan lied.

"Good stuff, I tell you. If you like weird stories and all."

They pulled onto 50th toward the zoo and wove around Woodland Park, and Nolan slumped back against the seat. The streets were darker here, the park closed. *And later in the hour, we've got a treat for you. Helmar Reiter, deep-sea linguist, will talk to us about teaching dolphins the alphabet.* There was more traffic now. He was almost home. "Two more lights, then hang a right," he said.

"Right about here someplace, that's where they saw them. One was a buck, I heard. Run right across four lanes at nine in the morning, then crashed into the Starbucks." The man whistled. "Cops had to shoot him. The others, they're still around here somewhere. Imagine surviving that every goddamned day of your life."

They waited at the light. Nolan could finally feel the booze. The light lasted forever. The man's hands clenched the wheel. Nolan couldn't stop staring at them, and the man noticed. He smiled. "I got a couple of bottles back at the ranch. Just a little ways from here. Not far at all and real quiet. What do you say?"

Nolan pushed at the handle, threw his weight at the door to get it open, but it wouldn't budge.

"Take it easy," the man said, but Nolan kept pushing. The light turned green. The man sped forward and took the next street, pulling over, shifting into park. "I got it," he said. "Hold on. Hold on."

The man pulled himself out of the car and wiggled the door open from the outside. "Get out you want out so bad."

Nolan climbed out. The man stood waiting, but Nolan couldn't look at him, couldn't even open his mouth to thank him. He started walking up the street, and then he broke into a run. He ran all the way up the hill and over three blocks until he got to Sigrid's condo and let himself in. In his room, the radio was still on, and he yanked the plug from the wall and got into bed without changing out of his clothes. The room was bright with the moon. He'd stay awake all night if he had to. He'd figure it out. Why he was so angry. Why even his own mother was braver than him. She'd gotten over something more horrific than he'd ever know in his whole damn life. He wanted to know how this was. How this could be when he couldn't even name what it was he was running from, and whether it was Wilkes that had made him this way. Arvel Wilkes standing over his crib and stroking a hand over Nolan's forehead, marking him a quitter or a survivor, Nolan didn't know which.

ADVICE FOR THE HAUNTED

ANY OTHER COUPLE WOULD HAVE THROWN AWAY THE FORMER owner's things and moved in, but two months after buying the apartment at auction, Nick and I were still using it as a playhouse. The former owner's name had been Natalia. We had "inherited" all of her possessions, her pantry and freezer stuffed with food. Under the couch, she had wedged bottles of cheap red wine. Nick joked that we could survive at Natalia's forever. "It's like our own private fallout shelter," he said, as we peeled back her bedspread and crawled under the sheets. We didn't concern ourselves with the circumstances of her death. We were young and in love, and the misfortunes of others had nothing to do with us.

The flat had one bedroom, an office, and a narrow kitchen that opened into a long central room. Heavy drapes shut out the city view. The furniture was outdated; the Persian rugs, threadbare and stained. The ceilings and walls had recently been spackled, leaving bone-white spots. On the buffet, next to the dining table, were stacks of postcards of paintings, many of them torn or chewed at the corners. We found a half-used bottle of anti-anxiety pills in the medicine cabinet, a glass accordion in a folded tablecloth, a baggie of foreign coins in a boot at the back of a closet. In a rickety piano bench, we discovered faded Polaroids of two girls at what looked like a family picnic.

We were still paying rent for our own apartments and rarely talked of the future. At Natalia's, we'd spend entire weekends pretending we were the last two people on Earth. We liked to camp it up. "Zombies?" I'd say.

"Meteorite." He'd tear off his tie. "It's at least three miles wide." Sunlight would be breaking through the drapes. "Do you see how dark it's getting?"

"What will we do?" I'd say, unbuttoning my blouse.

We ransacked her cupboards, pulled out soapstone animals from Africa. We placed the rhinoceros and giraffe in compromising positions. We played like children, pillaging her closets. Then we learned from the downstairs neighbor that Natalia had been a recluse who hadn't left the apartment in years. Something had happened to the sister who brought her supplies, and Natalia had started venturing into the hallway. One day she left the building with a suitcase and somehow plunged to her death from the L platform just two blocks away.

We continued to rearrange her furniture and tchotchkes. We still pretended we were secret agents or a strange new semi-human species that had survived the apocalypse. Entire weekends passed before we left the apartment or ate a real dinner, but we studied her photographs more closely now. We invented roles for Natalia in our games: captor, hostage, aunt.

Once or twice a week, Nick and I met at Natalia's during my lunch break. We were soaking in Natalia's tub. Nick handed me a mug of wine. "Don't look at me like that," he said. "You know you're not going back to work."

We thought it was a shame Natalia had had to bathe alone in such a wondrous tub. The guy beneath us had said that the morning of her death, she said hello to him in the hallway. "But she was all strange and spacey. Really happy, you know. The kind of happy people get before they jump."

"But the suitcase," I said to Nick. "He said she was carrying a suitcase. Why would she, if she was planning on ending it all?"

He pulled a long leg out of the water and slung it over the edge of the tub. "She should have never left," he said. "She had everything she needed right here."

I stood and reached for a towel. I'd been hearing noises, and what I heard then was the sound of a wrench knocking against metal inside the bathroom walls. The door creaked open and cold air rushed in. I hopped out of the tub and shut it, but as soon as I turned around, it opened again.

Nick crossed his arms over his chest and in a rich falsetto said, "Natalia, stay out. We're naked."

I laughed out loud, but then came a sound like steel marbles rolling across the ceiling. I think even Nick had the feeling we weren't alone. He handed me his mug. "Hold this," he said, and when I reached, I slipped on the tile and struck my head.

Nick got out and examined my forehead. "It's not that bad," he said. "Barely a scratch, but you're going to have a goose egg."

"Natalia did it," I said. I was only half-kidding.

We tightened our towels and made our way to the kitchen. I took a box of crackers and a jar of peanut butter from the cupboard. "I don't know what it is about this place that makes me so hungry," I said.

Nick dug into the peanut butter with a spoon. "It's that we didn't buy this food ourselves."

"No, it's like it's not real. Like there's no world out there."

"Precisely," he said. He pulled me close. "Let's never leave."

We joked about turning the apartment into a private country, a micronation like Christiania in Denmark. We'd call it the Republic of Natalia and design our own special stamp.

The next morning, I noticed an imprint in the bedding, as if someone had been sitting there watching us. Nick was in the kitchen paging through one of Natalia's books, and he showed it to me. "Classical mathematics," he said.

"No wonder she didn't have any friends."

"I thought you liked math." He filled one of the miniature cups from her china set with coffee and put it down in front of the extra stool at the breakfast bar. "Good morning, Nat," he said. "How'd you sleep?"

"She's grumpy in the morning," he said to me. "Doesn't like to talk." He winked.

"I think it's time to tell Oscar and Joelle," I said. "About the apartment, I mean."

Oscar and Joelle were our closest friends. They were the reason we were together. And Oscar believed in ghosts. He was a sort of amateur ghost hunter. I wanted to get his read on the place. "Let's have them over, for dinner or something."

"You know how Natalia feels about company," Nick said. "Besides, they don't have visas yet."

"I'm going to be late," I said.

Nick put the book aside and got up to make another pot of coffee. "We don't start before ten in the Republic of Natalia."

"Too bad I don't work for the Republic. If I keep this up, we won't be able to afford to live in the Republic anymore." I had intended the words more lightly.

"I never asked you to put up the down payment," he said. "It didn't need to be that large."

So far we had managed to mostly avoid talking about the purchase or my paying more toward the mortgage. I was in the middle of several large acquisitions at work, and any conversation about interest rates and balloon payments was likely to turn into an argument about corporate greed in the face of famine and war.

I left Nick in the kitchen and went to Natalia's closet to look for something to wear. We almost never stayed overnight during the week. I was traveling more for due diligence, always to other cities in the Midwest or the South. I was constantly shuttling between airports and hotels, between my own apartment, Natalia's, and my office downtown. I felt disoriented, and my excuses for leaving work were growing absurd.

Most of Natalia's clothes were outdated. I recognized a purple dress from a photograph of a much younger Natalia in front of a fountain with a boyfriend somewhere in Europe. We had propped the photo against a lamp on her dresser, and I looked at it again as I changed into the dress. The boyfriend had a goofy grin and thick hair that stuck up in a cowlick, and Natalia threw her head back to laugh. She must have been healthy then.

I searched her underwear drawer with dread, wishing I had brought an overnight bag. All of Natalia's undergarments were plain white cotton, many with frayed elastic. I reminded myself that Natalia was dead and wouldn't care if I wore something of hers, but I rejoiced when I found a lacy pair of silk panties that still had a price tag. I wondered when she had bought them, and why just one pair. I put them on and for a moment I was Natalia, untouched for too long.

At Fullerton, I waited on the platform for the Red Line. I checked my email on my phone, only partially aware of a pack of unruly school kids horsing around. One of them slammed into me. I stumbled toward the tracks, and an enormous woman grabbed me and pulled me back. I thought little of this until I was standing in the compartment and the woman pointed at my phone and said, "That thing's gonna be the death of you."

I squirmed against the sensation of the silk against my skin. "I'm wearing the underwear of a dead lady," I wanted to confess.

I arrived at work late for yet another meeting and made up an excuse about a mechanical problem delaying my train. It was a harmless lie, but I had told so many by then I had the uneasy feeling I would be fired.

After work that evening I went out to meet my running club. They were a rugged group that ran even when temperatures dipped below zero. I wanted to be like them. At the waterfront, I tried to keep up. Lake Michigan frothed, and gulls struggled against the wind. The man in front of me lagged too. He kept wiping his arm across his brow. He tripped and regained his balance, and then his legs buckled under him.

At first I thought he had simply slipped, but he wasn't moving and several other runners gathered around him. "I don't think he's breathing," a woman said. I stood looking on with the crowd, and then sirens sounded and before long a paramedic was pushing us back, saying, "Give us some room, folks." The others turned back, but I jogged another mile or two. I didn't know the man, and that's what I told myself all along the lake. *He's just a stranger. You don't know him. This sort of thing happens every day.*

I didn't want to be alone, so I called Nick and went to Natalia's. I pulled off my wet clothes and filled the bath. The refraction of my hands underwater made them appear broken off and reattached at the wrong angle. I ran my fingers over the welt on my forehead. I had fallen or almost fallen twice in less than 24 hours, and then, directly in front of me, a man had collapsed and probably died.

I got into bed, but not before putting the soapstone animals away in Natalia's dresser, not before turning on the bedside light and making sure my phone was within reach. I couldn't stop seeing the man at the lake, his legs giving way. I turned my face to the pillow and tried not to think of Natalia drooling into the same feathers.

Then Nick was standing in the bedroom doorway. He held his arms out and made his eyes dull, and I said, "Yes, please. Bring on the zombies."

He vaulted into bed and got under the covers, and I jolted at his cold hands. "You're so warm," he said. "God, you feel good," and then he was kissing me, we were turning together, the covers off now, tangled around our legs. I was kneeling in the middle of the bed, the two of us reflected in the mirror above the dresser. The drawer seemed to open a little more. Nick's arm tightened around my waist. He kissed the back of my neck.

The apartment walls were mere skin. The patched spot on the ceiling seemed to pulse. I closed my eyes to make it stop. Nick's breath was in my ear, and when I opened my eyes Natalia was there, hovering at the end of the bed. She was a blur, then her ashen face appeared, her mouth opened as if to scream, only it was me screaming, throwing Nick off me, and wrenching the covers to my chin.

"Who's there?" Nick said. He stared in the direction of the dresser for several minutes and then crept back into bed. We huddled together and slept.

We said nothing about what had happened until the next morning when Nick teased me about my pushing him off the bed.

"But you saw her. I know you did."

"I didn't see anything. I thought someone broke in. You're the one who screamed."

"Then why didn't you check the apartment? Why didn't you check the door?"

He didn't answer, just waved me away and went into the bedroom with his laptop to work.

He had canceled our meeting with a general contractor about the apartment remodel, claiming he had a deadline. He worked for an international relief organization and spent much of his time drafting reports and making overseas calls. Earlier in the year, two of his colleagues had been killed in a bombing, another taken captive. He had stopped reading the news, and when he mentioned work at all now it was to complain it was meaningless. I couldn't be certain, but I thought there were new cans of soup in the cupboard, that he was secretly adding to Natalia's stash and replenishing the store of wine under the couch. I found him staring into the mirror in the hallway talking to himself and thought I caught Natalia's name. I worried she had worked her way into him, that if we didn't do something soon, he'd be afraid to leave the apartment too.

What we needed was the company of friends, so I called Oscar and Joelle, and we met them at a nearby restaurant. It was almost like old times, the two of them telling such good stories. They were animated, flushed with life. They had a seven-year-old named Lucy and lived west of the city, and we hadn't seen them in months.

"We bought a condo," I blurted. "In Lincoln Park. Can you believe it?"

Nick pinched me under the table.

"It's about time," Joelle said. I noticed she wasn't drinking and suspected she was pregnant again. They had been trying for several years to have a second child, going through fertility treatments, suffering one loss after another.

"It's not official yet," Nick said, glancing at me. "Even if we do get it, it could be months before the whole thing's finalized."

"You couldn't pay me to live in Lincoln Park," Oscar said.

"It's small. Two bedrooms, one is barely big enough for an office," I said, trying to downplay how expensive it was.

"It's not that small," Nick said. "Whole families live with less."

"The woman who lived there killed herself," I said, and Nick buried his face in his hands. "It went into probate. All her stuff is still inside."

"How'd she do it?" Oscar asked.

Nick looked up at Oscar. "Don't even go there. It didn't happen in the apartment. And she didn't kill herself. She fell in front of a train. She tripped or something."

Oscar tore off another piece of bread and seemed to ponder it before wedging it into his mouth. "If you buy it, I'm bringing my equipment."

"I'm telling you, it's not haunted."

"Does this mean there might be a wedding?" Joelle asked.

"Not if Natalia has her way," I said.

"Natalia?" Oscar said. "You mean you knew this person?"

"No," Nick said. "Like I said, we're just thinking about buying it."

Nick barely spoke the rest of the evening and was silent as we walked back to the apartment. When we got inside he said, "Are you happy now?" He gestured all around. "Now Natalia's is going to be just like everywhere else."

"It *is* like everywhere else, Nick. It's just an apartment. You didn't have to lie to them."

"I can't believe I didn't see it."

"See what?" I asked. "Do you know how much money we've been wasting?"

"Yes," he said. "It's always about money, isn't it?"

*

The next morning I flew to Des Moines for work. When I tried calling Nick, he wouldn't answer. I returned to the apartment several days later, and the place was littered with plates of half-eaten pasta, crumpled paperwork, Natalia's CDs and albums. The carved animals marched in a parade down the hallway. The air smelled musty. All the drapes were pulled shut.

I opened the bedroom door and found Nick in bed, buried under a pile of blankets, a pillow over his head to block the light, the curtains blowing in cold air from the open window. I could just make out his whiskery chin. The armchair from the corner of the room was next to the bed, as if someone had been watching over him. The hair on my arms stood on end.

I pulled the pillow away and Nick blinked at me. "Hey," he said.

"Hey," I said, crawling under the covers. "Are you OK?"

"I can't sleep," he said. "The lights keep going on and off."

"They're probably doing electrical work somewhere in the building."

"Maybe," he said. "But what if Oscar was right? What if she's here?"

We called Oscar and by evening the apartment was rigged with cords and computers, with sensors and blinking red lights. Oscar had taken photos of Nick that showed a pinkish-red orb above his head. "See that?" he said. "Ectoplasm. You're definitely haunted, Nicky. But not as much as this place."

He found nothing in his photos of me. "Sorry, friend," he

said, patting my arm. "Don't take it personally. The women have always had a thing for Nick."

Nick and I slept at my apartment that night, and when we returned the next morning Oscar led us from room to room, indicating places of high activity. He was giddy with excitement. He showed us charts of energy fluctuations on his computer. "This is from the bedroom," he said, pointing to a jagged line of temperature shifts he found disturbingly erratic.

I wondered about cell towers, but said nothing. Then Oscar played a series of recordings of thumping and rattling and what sounded like someone opening and closing cupboards.

"We've heard that before," Nick said. "It's an old building."

"Then what do you make of this?" Oscar played a recording of a hollow, raspy voice saying what sounded like "Are you there?" and a second one that said, "Hurry. Hurry." Or maybe "Hurray. Hurray."

"Tell me you engineered that," Nick said.

I expected Oscar to laugh, but instead he looked at us gravely and said, "You started this, dudes. The lady's confused. You've got to get rid of her stuff. Every last thing. Throw her a going-away party or something. You've got to tell her it's time to leave."

It snowed the Friday of Natalia's party, the first major storm of the season. We had cleaned the apartment and made a spread of her food and drink. Nick was more energized than I had seen him in months. He talked about refinishing the floors. He talked about a lead on a new job with a better NGO. We poured bottles of Natalia's booze into an enormous punch bowl we found in her storage space in the basement, still in its original box. "If we're going to do this, let's really do it," Nick said. He filled each room with light from Natalia's emergency candles, and he made an altar of photos and figurines on the breakfast bar. He even went out and bought flowers for her, white chrysanthemums and roses.

"That's what I love about this guy," Oscar said. "He wants to make even the ghosts feel special."

He and Joelle had left Lucy with Oscar's mother and were staying overnight. Friends we hadn't seen in ages arrived, and we stood around drinking, catching up, looking at Natalia's photos. Oscar told ghost stories as he led them on a tour of the apartment.

In the kitchen, Joelle caught me staring at her drink.

"Two solid embryos. I really thought it was going to happen this cycle," she said. "Oscar wants to see a different doctor, but I think I'm done."

I tried to hug her, but she pulled away.

"This party must seem a little ridiculous right now," I said.

"Yes," she said. "But we could use a little ridiculousness."

Most of our guests were like Oscar and Joelle, exhausted parents unused to staying out late. We stood around sipping from plastic cups. Then more people arrived, and the mood grew lively. We celebrated until midnight, when Oscar positioned himself behind the makeshift altar. He waved Natalia's rhinoceros in the air and whistled loudly. Then Nick yelled, "Listen up, everyone. Let's at least give this a shot." Someone handed Nick a shot of whiskey, and he knocked it back and said, "Seriously, guys. Gather round."

Oscar asked Nick and me to remove the hallway mirror, and then he encouraged everyone to hold something of Natalia's. Someone placed a hand on the coffee table. Someone else, on the small oil painting Natalia must have gotten from a street vendor in Paris before she became ill. Joelle wrapped her hand around a floor lamp. A friend of Oscar's grabbed the photo of Natalia before the fountain.

"I ask you," Oscar said. His voice caught as he glanced at Joelle. "To silently help our friend Natalia let go of this world."

One of Nick and Oscar's old college pals said, "Oscar, you should have been a priest," and there was laughter, and then the room quieted again.

"It's time, Natalia. We're going to close the gateway now."

We held the mirror up facing the room. Oscar moved a candle closer and someone said, "Look," and everyone gasped, and I knew they had glimpsed her reflection.

Oscar held up his hand. "Be calm, everyone. Don't frighten her," and just then the floor lamp turned on and Joelle screamed and jumped back, and one of Oscar's friends yelled, "This is so staged."

"Natalia," Oscar said. "Stay with us. We're here to help you." He nodded at Nick and me to follow him to the sink. We carried the mirror like a coffin and rested it over the basin. Everyone crowded into the kitchen, and no one said a word. Nick filled his cupped hands with water and let it run over the surface.

"Tell her you're letting her go," Oscar said. "Tell her to cross over."

Nick looked up at everyone. "Wow," he said. "I can't believe I'm doing this." His voice came out soft at first and then louder as he said, "Natalia, can you hear me? There are a lot of people here for you."

Oscar nodded at him to continue. "Come on, Nicky. Tell her."

Nick said a few more words. He seemed flustered, and then resigned as he said, "I want you to look for the light and go into it. Don't be frightened." He stepped aside, and Oscar wrapped the mirror in a towel and set it next to the door to be gotten rid of with everything else.

"That's it," Oscar said. "Portal's closed. She's gone. I think."

Then he burned sage, and people coughed, and some went out to the balcony, and others to the bedroom to find their coats and leave.

Nick and I pressed pots and pans into people's arms. "Everything that's left is getting donated or thrown out. You want something, take it," we said.

We propped open the front door, said goodnight to those who were leaving, coerced them into taking extra dishes and trinkets. Furniture was hoisted and bumped down the stairs. The rugs, the postcards, the menagerie of animals, it was as if Natalia herself was being scattered throughout the city.

The downstairs neighbor came up to ask us to turn down the music, and we tried to give him a stack of old CDs. "No way," Oscar said, snatching them back. "Too close to home." The last of our guests left. A few lingered to talk in the stairwell. Then the apartment grew still. We had made up the bed for Oscar and Joelle, and Joelle stumbled to the bedroom to sleep. Oscar sat down on the floor, his equipment all around him. He had his digital recorder running again, attempting to pick up any lingering voices from the beyond. Nick and I bundled up and went to the roof to look out at the city. "It will be better now," I said, and he said, "It's weird, isn't it? To think of this as ours?"

When I woke that morning on the pullout couch, Oscar, Joelle, and Nick were already awake and in the kitchen eating doughnuts from the bakery down the street. Joelle handed me a cup of coffee in a paper cup. Oscar stood at the counter, playing part of a recording from the night before. "That," he said. "You didn't hear that? Listen again."

"I hear static, Oscar," Nick said, biting into a doughnut. "Just static."

Outside, rain turned to sideways sleet. We had scheduled a Salvation Army pickup for the next morning and had much to do. We threw the trash from the party down the garbage shoot. We set to work on the kitchen, emptying and cleaning the shelves and pantry, boxing the extra food. In the bedroom, we dismantled the bed and finished bagging the clothes.

"The mirror," I said, pointing to the one over the dresser. "We forgot this one."

Oscar looked alarmed. "Not to worry," he said. "We'll put it outside."

We lifted the dresser out the door and down the stairs to the curb. The sky had cleared. People hurried past on their way to the L and were momentarily reflected in the mirror. We said goodbye to Oscar and Joelle as we made our way back. I was sorry to see them go, even sorrier once we were back in the near-empty apartment. Without the rugs in the living room and hallway, every footstep on the wood floor echoed. The windows rattled. If anyone had looked up into our apartment just then, they would have seen us standing in a vacant room, lovers perhaps, on the verge of moving in or out. We were suddenly tired, and we went to the bedroom. We had yet to remove the curtains there, and Nick closed them. We spread blankets on the floor, kicked off our shoes and lay down. I tucked my head into Nick's shoulder, and we listened to the wind, to a helicopter whirring above the building on its way to the hospital.

"It's almost like she was never here," Nick said.

"Yes," I said, but it wasn't true.

We talked about the bright new things we would buy, the renovations we'd make. "I can't wait to tear out those soffits," I said. Nick shut his eyes, but I could tell he wasn't sleeping. I stared at the spackled spot on the ceiling, at the dull walls, and tried to imagine the room in a shade of yellow or blue. Tomorrow we'd go grocery shopping. We would only stock as much as we needed to get through a week or two, never more. We wouldn't hoard like Natalia had. We would throw parties and go out with our friends and never prepare for unknowable disasters. It would become an incantation, a theme song for the coming years. To never be like Natalia. To take the train downtown each morning. To never be afraid.

NOTES

"Felina" is inspired by the works of Louise Bourgeois, especially her 1980s series *Cells*.

The movie theater and café in "Notes to a Shadowy Man" is modeled after the historic Grand Illusion Cinema in Seattle.

The postcard painting referenced in "Boys on a Veranda" is Finnish artist Albert Edelfelt's 1890 painting *The Elköf Boys on the Veranda of Villa Sjökulla*.

The one unnamed film referenced in "A Habit of Seeing" is *Invasion of the Body Snatchers*.

The radio program in "How to Walk on Water" is inspired by the late Art Bell's *Coast to Coast AM*.

ACKNOWLEDGMENTS

This collection, written over many years, is stitched together with the invisible threads of readers, editors, and loved ones. I'm indebted to Chris Clemans for taking a chance on the early manuscript and helping me to strengthen it; to David Bowen and John McNally for bringing it to New American Press; to Alban Fischer and Jessica Miller for designing the cover and interior; to Mike Levine for providing a final read; and to my wise publicist Sheryl Johnston. Original versions of these stories were improved and published by Amie Barrodale, Sven Birkerts, Jason Brown, Jennifer Alise Drew, Toni Graham, Jim Hicks, Ellis Jones, David Lynn, Vern Miller, Speer Morgan, Michael Nye, William Pierce, Evelyn Somers, and Elizabeth Wagner.

I'm especially grateful for those who read early drafts of various stories, including Angela Ajayi, Judith Cooper, Glenn Deutsch, Eileen Favorite, Mikhail iossel, Aram Kim, T Kira Madden, Beth Marzoni, Melinda Moustakis, Jeff Parker, Adeena Reitberger, Emily Stinson, and Chris Sullivan. Many of these readers also provided other kinds of support, as did Maggie Anderson, Ada Calhoun, Adam Clay, Rebecca Entel, Edward Hamlin, Heather Jacobs, Colleen Kinder, Laura Harrison, Susan Neil, Jessi Phillips, Janaki Ranpura, Robin Rozanski, Heather Slomski, Christine Sneed, Mark Turcotte, and many others.

Special thanks to my parents and siblings, who helped to make me into a reader and a writer, and to my late father, who brought books home by the boxful and taught me that most wounds can be treated with a story.

Much of this manuscript was written while at Western Michigan University. I'm appreciative of my workshop mates and professors, especially my phenomenal and inimitable dissertation advisor, Jaimy Gordon, and Peter Blickle, Nancy Eimers, Robert Eversz, Richard Katrovas, Jil Larson, Lisa Cohen Minnick, Chris Nagle, William Olsen, Scott Slawinski, Gwen Tarbox, and Daneen Wardrop.

Many thanks to the following organizations that provided time and resources to complete this book: The Rona Jaffe Foundation, MacDowell Colony, The Ragdale Foundation, and Summer Literary Seminars.

This book would be impossible without the love and encouragement of my husband John Balbach. This book is dedicated to him, and to ZZ, Calvin, and Aloysius.

RACHEL SWEARINGEN's stories and essays have appeared in *VICE*, *The Missouri Review*, *Kenyon Review*, *Off Assignment*, *Agni*, *American Short Fiction*, and elsewhere. She is the recipient of the 2015 Missouri Review Jeffrey E. Smith Editors' Prize in Fiction, a 2012 Rona Jaffe Foundation Writers' Award, and the 2011 Mississippi Review Prize in Fiction. In 2019, she was named one of 30 Writers to Watch by the Guild Literary Complex. She holds a BA from the University of Wisconsin–Madison and a PhD from Western Michigan University, and teaches at the School of the Art Institute in Chicago.